THE *RAVAGERS*

DONALD HAMILTON

A **MATT HELM** NOVEL

THE **RAVAGERS**

TITAN BOOKS

The Ravagers
Print edition ISBN: 9781781162309
E-book edition ISBN: 9781781162378

Published by Titan Books
A division of Titan Publishing Group Ltd
144 Southwark Street, London SE1 0UP

First edition: February 2014
1 2 3 4 5 6 7 8 9 10

A CIP catalogue record for this title is available from the British Library.

Printed and bound in the United States.

THE **RAVAGERS**

1

It was an acid job, and they're never pleasant to come upon, even when you're more or less prepared to find something wrong, as I'd been. One of our people had failed to call in when he was supposed to, and I'd been pulled off another job nearby—well, five hundred miles south in the Black Hills of South Dakota—and sent up to investigate. I'd crossed the border into Canada well after dark, I'd found the right motel, named The Plainsman, in the right town, named Regina, in the right province, named Saskatchewan, and I'd given the right knock on the door and received no answer.

Following instructions, I had then circumvented the lock with a special piece of plastic disguised as a credit card, slipped inside, and waited in the dark for a reasonable length of time, to see if anybody cared to jump me or shoot at me. Nobody had. Hearing nothing breathe or move in the room, I'd turned on the light and seen him lying on the floor at the foot of the bed.

It wasn't pretty. I don't monkey with the stuff myself. Not many professionals do, although I have met a few—on both sides—who felt there was nothing like a splash of nice corrosive chemical reagent to make the most stubborn subject forget his principles and talk, if that was needed. For quick information, they'd claimed, it beat the thumbscrews and hot pokers all hollow. And as a distraction in a tight spot it was a natural, since people weren't apt to give much trouble while being painfully consumed alive.

On the other hand, acid is messy, risky to keep around, and hard to use without getting some on yourself; and the resulting burns, on flesh or clothing, are distinctive and hard to explain away. So we generally leave it to the jealous ladies who want to spoil their rivals' looks. But it had been used here, liberally and viciously. It had made brownish charred splotches on the pale motel carpet, and it had pretty well destroyed the face of the man I'd come here to check up on.

At least I thought he was the man I'd come to find, but it was a little hard to tell. He wasn't a colleague I'd ever known well, although we'd worked together briefly a couple of times, and the visible part of his face bore little resemblance to what I recalled of the agent we knew as Gregory, normally a wavy-haired, clean-cut, American-boy type who specialized in the gigolo bit and other techniques requiring youthful masculine charm. The hands, which had presumably gone up in a vain attempt to shield the face, were also seared and blistered almost beyond recognition.

He lay half across his own suitcase, which he'd pulled off the stand at the foot of the bed—or somebody had arranged things to look that way. His belongings were scattered about the floor, as if he'd flung them aside crazily, feeling for something in the bag with his burning hands. Or maybe, blinded and in agony, he'd simply lost his way, fallen over the luggage stand, and thrashed around deliriously, trying to make the bathroom to wash the fiery stuff off…

I'd stepped away from the switch, crouching, after getting light into the room. Now I straightened up slowly, but I didn't really relax, nor did I put away the little .38 Special revolver I'd neglected to declare at customs when crossing the border. First I made quite sure the room was uninhabited except by me and the motionless figure on the rug. Then I checked the closet and found it unoccupied. That left the bathroom. I stepped over Greg and made my entry in the manner recommended by the training manual. I determined that this cubicle was also empty except for the shiny new US-style plumbing. I drew a long breath, put the gun away, made sure the door to the outside world had latched properly, and returned to kneel beside Greg.

He'd been dead long enough to feel cold to the touch. Well, it takes a certain amount of time to drive five hundred miles, even with your foot flat on the floor. The acid used had been sulfuric—oil of vitriol—I judged from the fact that it gave off no seriously annoying fumes. Most of the others will set you coughing when they're concentrated enough to do that much damage.

There was a small prescription bottle by his right hand. The name on the label was Michael Green, the name he'd been using. The directions read: *Take one (1) at bedtime if needed for sleep.* The cap was off and the contents were missing except for a couple of yellow capsules that had got spilled among the tumbled clothing: probably the sedative known as nembutal. If you want to sound hep, you can call them yellow-jackets.

I frowned at the dead man. Apparently I—or the Canadian policeman who'd investigate this—was supposed to think that after the acid attack Greg had gone groping for his sleeping pills to kill himself, as an escape from blindness, disfigurement, and intolerable agony. I didn't believe it for a moment. Not that Greg might not have reacted in this general way—he'd been vain about his good looks—but it takes a lot of barbiturate to kill and quite a lot of time, and we carry much more effective tickets to oblivion. I made a quick search and found his, never mind where. That's a business secret, but the significant thing was that, having handy on his person a little pill that would give him death in a few seconds, if that was what he wanted, he'd hardly have gone to the trouble of tearing apart his suitcase for a clumsy substitute.

It followed that, since acid burns don't generally bring death—and then only slowly—unless very large skin areas are affected, and since making a man dripping with acid swallow a large quantity of sedative capsules isn't really practical, the vitriol thrower must have finished the job by other means. I could see no signs of direct physical violence, so he'd probably used something poisonous, tricky, hard to detect, and impossible to trace. To hell with that. I'd been sent to check on Greg, not to get caught here playing detective around his dead body.

I got up and looked around. Washington would want me to clean up as much as possible, I decided, to make the cover-up easy if it was to be bandied that way. I already had the little death pill that, if discovered at the autopsy, would have revealed that Greg was something other than the innocent U.S. tourist he'd been pretending to be. There was nothing else in the room that wasn't strictly in character. Well, there wouldn't be. He'd been a little too cocky to be one of my favorite people, but there had never been any doubt that Greg was a pro, which made it all the more peculiar, his getting caught like this.

As I moved toward the door, I saw something white under a chair close by, and picked it up: a woman's white kid glove. At least it had been nice and white once. Now it was stained with brown and some other odd colors where the acid had reacted only partially with the soft, expensive leather.

I put the glove into my pocket, hoping it wouldn't eat a hole there, and slipped out into the night, silent and, I hoped, unseen.

2

Regina is a good-sized Canadian town on the great plains some hundred miles north of the border. You couldn't tell it from a U.S. prairie city if it weren't for the billboards advertising Canadian brands you never heard of—that is, in addition to such international commodities as Coke and Chevrolet. The money, I had already discovered, is Canadian dollars and cents, currently worth between five and ten per cent less than the equivalent U.S. currency; and the filling stations sell gasoline by the imperial gallon, which has five quarts instead of four. It makes your car's gas mileage look terrific until you catch on.

The night was dark and starless, with a misty promise of rain that put haloes around the neon lights of the motel and the street lights beyond. I strolled away casually, like a man with nothing on his mind and time on his hands. The little Volkswagen I'd been using in the Black Hills was parked a couple of blocks away. It was apparently the car you got these days if you were west of the Mississippi and east of California and needed four wheels for official purposes. We're not a big government agency and the budget is limited, so they can't keep the latest air-conditioned Cadillacs and racing Ferraris spotted around the world for our convenience, although it would be nice.

I was familiar with this particular VW, having used it on an assignment farther south the year before. It had changed color and license since then—it was now painted black instead of pale blue, and it had Colorado instead of Arizona plates—but either the odometer had been set back or it hadn't seen much use in the intervening months: it had been in good shape when I picked it up in Denver to drive north to Rapid City, S.D.

Now, still farther north by some five hundred hasty miles, I settled myself deliberately behind the wheel, switched on, and spent a few seconds listening to the engine critically. The one thing those little Volkswagen fours won't take is being strenuously over-revved, and I hadn't lifted my foot much on the way here, not even on the downgrades. But the mill just made its usual healthy outboard-motor racket. I maneuvered out of the parking space and drove away, jazzing the throttle a bit from time to time and cocking my head to listen—acting the part of a man whose troubles, if any, were strictly mechanical.

I didn't check the rearview mirror too often, and I was careful not to look around. If anyone had followed me from the motel, I didn't want to scare him off. I wanted to bring him right along with me until I had instructions telling me what to do with him. Or her.

I found a phone booth at the corner of a shopping center parking lot. The stores were closed at this hour, the lot was empty, and I could stand at the phone undisturbed and watch the street casually through the glass of the booth while waiting for my call to go through. If there was anything significant about any of the cars that passed, I didn't spot it. "Eric here," I said, when I heard Mac's voice on the line. My real name, if it matters, is Matthew Helm, and at the moment I was going under the name of David Clevenger—at least I had been, on the other job—but we use the code names for official conversation.

Two thousand miles, and one international border away, Mac said, "Well?"

I made a face at the Volkswagen standing under the lights of the empty parking lot. "Have you got your red pencil handy, sir?"

"Go on."

"Scratch Agent Gregory. Our charm boy's had it."

There was a brief silence at the other end of the line, then Mac said flatly: "I see. Details?" I gave them to him, and he said: "Describe the glove."

"White kid, dressy, somewhat damaged. No manufacturer's or retailer's labels. No size marked, but it wasn't worn by a midget. The lady has long, slim, artistic fingers—or maybe just big, strong ones, it's hard to tell. Assuming, of course, that the glove was bought for the person who wore it tonight."

Mac said, "There is always the possibility of a frameup, but in this case it is unlikely."

"Well, you know more about the over-all situation than I do, sir."

"You will take over," Mac said. "The woman with whom we're dealing is five feet seven and a fraction inches tall, not an Amazon, but big enough to be eligible, I should think, as the advertising gentlemen would say, glove-wise. I can think of no other female candidate at the moment. She is heading east, accompanied by a young girl, her daughter. She is driving a pickup truck, pulling a house trailer."

I said, "That makes her a Westerner, born or transplanted. No delicate eastern flower would be caught dead in a truck."

"She has been living in the state of Washington for several years—at the White Falls Project on the Columbia River. You may have heard of it. Her husband is an eminent scientist attached to the project."

I said, "The picture is becoming clearer. Slowly."

"Gregory was supposed to make her acquaintance on the road and gain her confidence. However, she was on her guard and his reports indicate that beyond a speaking acquaintance he had so far got nowhere."

"If he'd got nowhere, why was he killed?" I asked.

"That is a very good question," Mac said dryly. "Perhaps you can find an answer."

"There's one catch, sir. My instructions emphasized speed. Secrecy was not, I gathered, of primary importance.

You wanted to know why he hadn't called on schedule, as soon as possible. To find out, I had to enter the motel room. There was no way of doing it without being seen, if anyone was watching. And if anyone was, he's probably got his eye on me now. Or she has. At least a connection between Greg and me may have been established."

Mac said, "If it has, it's unfortunate, but perhaps you can work out a cover story to account for it. Did I remember to ask you to bring along the camping equipment you were using in the Black Hills?"

"Yes, sir."

"Well, you will find your subject a few miles east of Regina on the Trans-Canada Highway, in a campground provided by the state—that is, the Province. Check trailer space number twenty-three. It should contain a blue Ford truck and a silver trailer. Here are the vehicle license numbers, state of Washington." He read them off. "If they are still there, have yourself assigned a camping space and stay the night. Check with me in the morning for further instructions."

"And if they're gone?"

"Report back immediately. We may be able to re-locate them for you. Incidentally, the woman's name is Drilling. Genevieve Drilling."

I said, "Nobody's named Drilling. That's making a hole where there wasn't any. Or it's a special kind of three-barreled gun."

Mac ignored my feeble attempt at levity. "The daughter's name is Penelope. She is fifteen years old and wears glasses for myopia and has braces on her teeth. Apparently mother and daughter were staying over a day in Regina to see a dentist for some minor adjustments."

"Um," I said. "Spectacles and orthodontal braces. A real little Lolita."

"The husband and father is Dr. Herbert Drilling, physicist. Mrs. Drilling has left his bed and board, and is presumed to be joining, sooner or later, a man of considerable physical attraction and questionable political affiliations calling himself Hans Ruyter. We have encountered Mr. Ruyter before under other names. Not really first-team material, but competent."

I sighed. "Don't tell me. Let me guess. Could it be that Mrs. Drilling just happened to latch onto a few scientific documents of national importance belonging to hubby, as she went out the door to meet her lover?"

"I'm afraid it could be and is."

I said, "My God! The old secret-formula routine. How corny can we get? I suppose it deals with some kind of nuclear-power super-gizmo? That's what they're doing up there on the Columbia, as I recall."

Mac said, "As a matter of fact, Dr. Drilling's specialty is lasers, if you know what that is."

I whistled softly. "Laser-maser. The latter-day death ray; disciplined light waves or something. Okay, so it's important, but how did we get roped into this one, sir? We're not the national lost-and-found agency. J. Edgar Hoover's boys are real sharp on stolen documents, I'm told, and so are the members of several other agencies.

What's so special about this particular batch of misplaced cellulose that they have to call on the wrecking crew, the hit-them-below-the-belt department, to find it?"

Mac said, "You are jumping to conclusions, Eric. Have I instructed you to find any documents?"

"Oh. Pardon me."

"There are some rather tricky matters involved," Mac said. "It seems to be a large and complex operation, only part of which concerns us. After you've looked over the ground and the people, I will give you the details, as far as they've been entrusted to us. Right now you had better get out there and check the campground while I get on the telephone and try to pull a few international strings to make sure Gregory's body is discovered by somebody discreet and official."

"Yes, sir," I said.

"Study the woman, and at the same time determine whether or not you are in the clear. If not, try to learn who is watching you. Do nothing hasty, however. Unfortunately we are not alone in this, if you know what I mean."

"I know," I said. "I hope they know it, too. There's nothing I hate like being shot by my friends."

"It's a chance you will have to take," Mac said. "As a matter of fact, other agencies have not been informed of our participation, and are not to be informed. Do you understand?"

"Yes, sir," I said, because it was the easiest thing to say, not because it was the truth.

She moved over to the Ford pickup, got in, pulled the tail of her garment in after her, closed the door, and cranked up the windows. She sat there for a while. The truck was parked looking my way. The night was too dark for me to make out her features through the windshield glass, let alone her expression, but I could see enough to know when she suddenly buried her face in her hands and bent over the steering wheel, obviously crying. Well, anybody can cry, and a woman who had recently committed a brutal murder might well want to have her reaction out where her child couldn't see her and ask why.

I reminded myself that it wasn't proved that Mrs. Genevieve Drilling had killed anybody, and that I wasn't here to prove it. From Mac's instructions, I deduced that I was supposed to gain the lady's trust and confidence for some altogether different purpose, as yet undisclosed. The fact that she could break down and cry was a promising sign. It indicated that an absorbent male shoulder might not be altogether unwelcome, if properly presented.

I suppose this was a coldblooded way of regarding a fellow-human in distress, a woman in tears. If I hadn't been cold and damp and cramped, lying there, I might have been ashamed of myself. As it was, I just wished she'd blow her nose and switch on a light so I could get a real look at her, and then climb back into her little tin box on wheels so I could leave without being spotted...

A sound behind me drove these unprofessional thoughts from my mind. There was a faint rustling and scuffling back there, indicating that I no longer had this part of the grove to myself. Somebody else was crawling up to take a peek. Then that person was suddenly quiet, as Mrs. Drilling got out of the truck and moved back to the trailer. She drew a sleeve across her eyes, reached up to pat her hair smoothed, squared her shoulders, opened the door, and made her way inside, leaving me still without a clear impression of her face and figure.

I lay very still. She'd said it was starting to rain. It hadn't been when she said it, but it was now. The sound of raindrops was a murmur all through the woods, but I could hear the man behind me get up and move away. Cautiously, I turned myself around and squirmed after him. The rain helped, making the dead leaves soft and silent and helping to cover any noise I made, but after a little of it I wasn't so sure I wouldn't have preferred to crawl on dry ground and take my chances.

The man ahead of me seemed to be fairly tall, and he moved like a reasonably young man, but he was either bald or very blond and crewcut: I could see his bare head gleaming faintly in the darkness even when I couldn't distinguish the outlines of his body. He wasn't much good in the woods. He made plenty of noise and he didn't seem to be quite sure where he was going. After a while he stopped in a baffled way, looking around. He whistled softly.

Another man spoke up from some bushes to the left. "Over here, Larry. Well?"

"Christ, I'm soaked. This is a cold damn country."

"Who cares about you? What about the woman?"

"She's still with us. I guess she's too smart to attract attention by pulling out after paying to stay the night. She was sitting out in the truck for some reason. Looked like she was crying." The tall man laughed scornfully. "Remorse, do you figure? Jeez, what a job she did on that poor guy's face, if it was she."

"If you hadn't let them slip away from you we'd know for sure."

"Hell, they were at the dentist! Who ever got away from a dentist in less than an hour?"

The unseen man said, "I wonder where the dead guy fits in, hanging around her. Well, fit. I guess he fits in nothing but a coffin, now. A closed coffin." I heard him get up. "Now that we've put her to bed, we'd better get on the phone and let them know the party's getting rough. Come on."

I gave the pair plenty of time to get clear. That made me thoroughly drenched by the time I'd crept back to check on the trailer again. Apparently Mrs. Drilling had found the crying jag relaxing. She wasn't moving around in there any more. I decided it was safe to leave her until morning, while I dried myself off and tried to find something to eat. My last meal had been a drive-in hamburger a couple of hundred miles south. My last sleep had been further away than that, but sleep, of course, means nothing to us iron men of the undercover professions. At least that's the theory on which we're supposed to operate.

It was a segregated campground: the peasants with tents were separated from the aristocrats with trailers. I'd been assigned a space pretty well over to the other side of the wooded area, and I'd pitched my tent to establish my claim before sneaking off to play Indian in the brush. The little Volkswagen was parked facing the front of the tent. From a distance it looked very good to me: it looked like dry clothes and a chocolate bar to ward off starvation until something more substantial could be obtained.

As I moved closer, however, the car suddenly began to look less good. There was somebody in it, a woman, by the hair. My first thought was that somehow the woman I'd been watching had beat me here—after all, I knew of no other woman in the case. Then she saw me coming and got out to meet me, and I saw that she was considerably smaller and wirier than Genevieve Drilling.

She stood by the car, waiting for me to reach her. I could make out that she was wearing dark pants and a light trench coat and light gloves. Her hair seemed to be black or very dark. Waiting, she pulled up a kind of hood to protect it from the rain.

"You're Clevenger?" she said as I stopped in front of her. "That's what it says on the registration. David P. Clevenger, of Denver, Colorado."

"That's me," I said. "Now let's talk about you."

"Not here," she said. "The Victoria Hotel, room four-eleven. Just as soon as you get cleaned up. You can't go through the lobby that muddy."

"The Victoria Hotel," I said. "What makes you think I'll come?"

She smiled. She seemed to have nice white teeth; they

showed up well in the darkness. I had the impression she might look quite attractive if I could see her clearly.

"Oh, you'll come," she said. "Or would you rather tell the Regina police what you were doing in a room at The Plainsman Motel with a dead body? Of course, the body had been dead for quite a while before you sneaked up and picked the lock to get in, but I don't really think you want to be called upon to explain your behavior officially, in a foreign country. Room four-eleven, Mr. Clevenger."

I said, "Throw in a drink and a roast beef sandwich and it's a deal."

She laughed and turned away. It was a break of sorts, I thought wryly, watching her walk off. Without expending any effort, I'd learned that I had, after all, been observed earlier. I was now taking steps to identify the observer, as I'd been instructed to do.

4

She was standing at the dresser in the corner, operating on the cap of an interesting-looking bottle, when I entered the hotel room after knocking on the door and being told it was unlocked, come in.

"Your sandwich is over on the TV," she said without looking around. "Help yourself, Mr. Clevenger. I'm sorry, they didn't bring up any mustard or catsup."

I said, "Who needs it? At the moment I could eat the damn cow with the hair on."

I went over and took a couple of bites and felt stirrings of returning strength and intelligence. I swung around to look at the small, wiry girl across the room. She was wearing slim black pants, a long-sleeved white silk shirt, and a little open black vest. What the costume was supposed to represent wasn't immediately clear to me, but then there's a lot about women's fashions I don't dig.

I asked, "Do I call you by a name or do you answer to any loud noise?"

She said without turning her head, "I'm registered as Elaine Harms. If you've got to call me something, that'll do."

"Sure."

"I hope you like Scotch. It's as cheap as anything up here, which isn't cheap."

"Scotch is fine."

Normally I'm a bourbon-and-martini man, but I don't consider it a principle worth fighting for at three in the morning in a strange girl's hotel room. Anyway, I was less interested in her liquor than in the face she was being so careful to hide from me. When she turned, there was something deliberate and challenging in the movement that would have warned me, had I needed warning. She came forward with a drink in each hand and a rather malicious gleam in her eyes, watching me for signs of shock. To hell with her. I've played poker since I was a boy; and I've seen plenty of men—and women, too— with damaged faces. Only a couple of hours back I'd seen a man with no face at all. She couldn't scare me.

I took the glass she held out and said, "Thanks. You're a lifesaver, Miss Harms."

"I hope your sandwich is all right, Mr. Clevenger."

"Swell," I said. "Two more like it would just about bring my day's intake up to the subsistence level."

It wasn't really very shocking. I mean, she'd had smallpox as a kid, that was all. It had left her skin with a general over-all roughness. It was too bad, of course, but not as bad as if she'd had the fragile type of good looks to which a rose-petal complexion is essential.

Instead, she had a kind of street-urchin face with a good big mouth and a small upturned nose. With a smooth skin, she'd merely have looked cute; now she looked both cute and tough. The smallpox scars did for her what a dueling scar does for a man; they gave her a hard and dangerous look. In her pants and silk shirt, she resembled one of the deadly, often similarly pockmarked, sword-packing young dandies of centuries past, who'd skewer you as soon as look at you.

She said, "You sound as if you'd come a long way fast, without taking time to stop and eat."

"I was down in South Dakota at noon today. Well, yesterday."

"What brought you up here?"

"A phone call," I said. "A phone call about a stupid jerk who might have got himself into trouble." I had worked out some kind of a story, driving over here, utilizing as much of the truth as I safely could. "I was supposed to wipe his nose and send him home to daddy."

"Who and where is daddy?"

I shook my head. "You want a lot for a roast beef sandwich, Miss Harms."

She persisted: "What was your connection with Mike?"

I didn't know what she'd been told by Greg. I gambled and said, "We were in the same line of business."

"He claimed to be an insurance man from Napa, California. He said he was on vacation, just a tourist."

I said, "I've got a card somewhere that says I sell insurance in Trinidad, Colorado. If you believe it, you're dumber than I think. If you believed Mike, you're dumber than I think."

"But you aren't saying what you really do?" When I didn't answer, she said, "We aren't getting very far, are we?"

"I've got no place to get," I said. "I'm just here because I was invited."

She studied me thoughtfully. After a little, she said, "The redcoats are attacking Bunker Hill, Mr. Clevenger."

I don't suppose that makes much sense to you, in the context, but it made a few things clear to me. It was her way of telling me who she was and asking me to identify myself similarly, if I could. From time to time somebody makes a hopeful attempt to correlate all the various undercover activities of our vast and unwieldy government, to make sure that they synchronize properly, and that nobody unwittingly sticks a thumb in a colleague's eye. It doesn't work out very well, for several reasons, one being that no cynical and experienced agent is going to be happy entrusting his life and mission to the irresponsible cretins working for some other department. Half the time we don't even trust the people in our own outfit.

This girl was not one of ours. Mac would have told me if there was someone around I could call upon for assistance. That made her a member of another agency, and now I was supposed to give her a brotherly kiss of recognition and say something about waiting till we saw the whites of their eyes—that isn't the countersign we were actually using, of course; but the real one was on about the same level of corniness. They all are.

According to official theory, Miss Harms and I would then sit down and compare notes about the Drilling operation in an atmosphere of mutual trust and confidence, and work out a plan for a joint campaign. You can see how the idea might appeal to a bunch of Washington efficiency experts who'd never been asked to stake their lives on some unknown character's reliability, on the strength of a widely distributed phrase that could easily have been compromised.

I said, "You've lost me, doll. Anyway, it was really Breed's Hill, wasn't it?"

I won't say whether, under other circumstances, I would have given the correct response. Normally, we're told to cooperate within reason, but it's left to the discretion of the agent on the spot and it's always a ticklish diplomatic question. In this particular case, of course, I had my orders. Mac had put it quite plainly: *Other agencies have not been informed of our participation, and are not to be informed.*

Elaine laughed quickly. "I'm sorry. I guess my mind was wandering." She hesitated. "Well, would you mind just telling me what you're doing here?"

I said, "Sure I'd mind." She started to speak, and I interrupted: "Now don't go threatening me again with the Regina cops, Miss Harms. I bet you don't want cops any more than I do. If you want to know about me and my business, tell me who's asking. If you were to show me a little gold badge, for instance, my attitude could change very suddenly."

She frowned. "What makes you think I—"

I said, "Why don't we try operating on the assumption that we're both reasonably bright people, for a change? That was a password or something you just tried on me, wasn't it? That Bunker Hill crap. So, since you seem to want a lot of questions answered, suppose you first tell me who you are, and why you've been watching a room that's got a dead man in it, and following people who entered that room, and checking them out with corny countersigns. If it's Uncle Whiskers who wants information, I might oblige. If it's Little Red Riding Hood, or Smokey the Bear, to hell with them."

She smiled faintly. "You're getting very tough all of a sudden, Mr. Clevenger."

I regarded her for a moment longer; then I swallowed the last of the sandwich and washed it down with the last of the drink and set the glass on the television set. I took two Canadian dollar bills from my wallet and laid them beside the glass.

"There you are," I said. "Nobody's obligated to nobody. If there's any change, give it to your home town Community Chest. I see you've got a phone, so you'll have no trouble calling the cops after I'm gone." I grinned at her and headed for the door. "See you in jail."

"Mr. Clevenger."

I stopped with my hand on the knob. "If it's got a question mark at the end of it, you're wasting your breath."

"I *am* working for the United States government, Mr. Clevenger. Uncle Whiskers, if you prefer."

I turned around. She had seated herself on the big double bed. As I came back across the room, she watched me closely for clues to what my reaction would be.

I went to stand over her and said grimly, "Well, I sure had to put on a big act to get that out of you, doll. Now show me something that says it besides you, and we're in business."

She shook her head. "We don't all carry little gold badges, Mr. Clevenger."

"I'm supposed to take your word for it?" I let her brace herself for an argument; then I shrugged. "Well, okay. I'm not hard to get along with. You come part way, I'll come part way. Maybe we'll get together eventually. I work for Western Investigation Services, 3001 Palomas Drive, Denver, Colorado."

She looked surprised. "A private detective?"

"That's right. Private investigator, private op, private eye, shamus, snooper, you name it."

"Can you prove it?"

I said, "You give proof, honey, you get proof. If your word's good, so's mine."

She laughed. "That doesn't necessarily follow."

I said, "Hell, it's easy enough to check, if you're really a government girl. All you have to do is pick up that phone and ask for long distance. Washington will have the dope back for you in the time it takes us to have another drink, if your bureaucracy's halfway on the ball."

She made no move toward the telephone; she didn't even look that way. She kept her eyes hard on me and said, "And Mike Green was a private investigator, too? You said he was in the same line of business."

She could have been leading me into a trap with the question. I gambled on the fact that Greg had been, for all his faults, a pro: he wasn't likely to have spilled any beans to a G-girl in pants.

"Sure," I said. "He worked for a West Coast outfit. They sometimes handle stuff for us out there, and vice versa, so when they called us for help my boss contacted me in Rapid City, where I was winding up some business, and told me to get the hell up here. Mike hadn't called his Los Angeles office when he was supposed to. They'd got worried and asked if we'd discreetly find out what was wrong." I grimaced. "They've got some weird notions of geography, out there in L.A. I think they figure anything east of the Rockies must be close to anything else east of the Rockies."

Elaine stared at me searchingly for several seconds; then she looked away and made herself comfortable on the bed. I wondered idly about the way women must be constructed differently from men, that makes them so happy sitting on their own feet. She looked up abruptly, hoping to catch me by surprise, I guess.

"Mike never gave me a hint of anything like this," she said. I didn't say anything, and she went on: "Of course, he did act pretty mysterious at times. I knew he wasn't just an insurance salesman seeing the sights. What was his interest in Mrs. Drilling? What's yours?"

I said truthfully, "I don't know yet."

"You're not denying that you're watching the woman, are you? After all, I saw you."

"Sure," I said. "I called Denver about Mike, and the boss sent me right out to check the camp for Drilling, to make sure she hadn't flown. He's contacting the coast to find out what the score is. I'll talk with him again in the morning." I frowned down at Elaine. "I don't suppose you'd care to tell me what kind of government business brings you here, Miss Harms."

She hesitated only briefly. "I don't see why not. You can pass the information along to your employer, with a word of warning. Mrs. Drilling has stolen some scientific documents of national importance. Her husband, scientist at a certain government project, apparently was a little careless with his briefcase at home. We are trying to get the contents back before she passes them to her lover, a man we know to be a foreign agent. We think she has made arrangements to join him somewhere in eastern Canada and escape with him overseas. We're also kind of interested in taking him, if it can be done without jeopardizing the main job, which is getting the papers back."

I said, "I suppose she's got rid of the stuff temporarily, or all you'd have to do is shake down her trailer and truck."

"As a matter of fact," Elaine said, "a thorough search was made, more or less surreptitiously and illegally I'm afraid, a couple of days ago. Nothing was found. She had three days to dispose of it after she left home, before she was located up in British Columbia. We think she must have mailed it to herself at some eastern address, and that she's now heading to pick it up. Anyway, we'll keep a close eye on her until we find it." Elaine looked up at me. "And you can tell your boss that any private agency that interferes is going to find itself in serious trouble."

I sighed. "Honey, you are the threateningest girl I ever did meet. First it was the Regina police and now, I suppose, it's the whole U.S. government. But I'll tell him. I'm sure he'll shake like a leaf. He's a very timid man, just like me."

The girl on the bed laughed. It was the first real, honest laugh I'd seen her give. It changed her face so you forgot the ways in which it missed perfection. She was really quite a nice-looking girl.

"I'm sorry," she said. "I didn't mean to sound pompous and official, but Mike Green caused us a lot of worry, hanging around the subject the way he did. We had to waste a lot of time on him, not knowing who he was."

"You didn't happen to see his murderer, while you were wasting all this time?"

She flushed slightly, as if I'd accused her of inefficiency, which of course I had. "No," she admitted. "No, when I got there this afternoon, he was already dead. But is there much doubt? I mean, there's only one logical candidate, isn't there?"

I said, "I wouldn't know. My information is limited. Well, I'll pass the warning word along when I talk to my boss in the morning. Now I'd better get out to camp and try to grab a few hours' sleep. My God, it's still raining! I hope I left the bedroll where it's dry. My tent isn't as waterproof as it might be." I glanced at my watch. "There's hardly enough of the night left to make it worth while blowing up that damn air mattress."

"You have a few hours yet. The Drilling woman hardly ever hits the road before nine o'clock." Elaine hesitated. Something in her attitude made me look at her sharply. She returned my look without expression, and patted the chenille spread on which she sat. "It's a big bed," she said.

It was one of those funny moments. The atmosphere of the room changed abruptly. She met my look with one that was half defiant, half challenging.

"It's a lonely damn profession," she said. I continued not to say anything. It was her party. She said, "Of course, if you'd rather not, okay. I mean, if you're being true to a wife or girlfriend, far be it from me to lead you astray. And if you only sleep with girls with peach-blossom complexions—" She stopped there, watching me.

I said, "And if I just happen to be tired from driving five hundred miles in eight hours? Those VWs aren't designed for road racing, you know."

Something changed in her eyes, turning them dull and opaque, like slate. "Well, it's as good an out as any," she said evenly. "Pardon me for being forward. Check with me in Brandon this evening. In case you forget the name, it's a town with a big provincial prison nearby. It's about a day's run east for Drilling unless she changes her driving habits drastically. Miss Elaine Harms. The Moosehead

Lodge, Room 14. I'll be waiting to hear from you. You'd better come up with the name of your principal and some good reasons for butting into this case. My chief isn't fond of private interference."

"Threats, always the threats," I said. I looked down at her and asked bluntly, "Did Mike Green ever get a similar invitation, and what was his response?"

She sat very still, cross-legged on the bed. There was a brief pause before she answered. "Mr. Green liked dames with looks and class," she said then, in a flat voice. "He wasn't about to lay any pockmarked monkeys when there was better stuff to be had, end of quote. Well, at least he was honest. He didn't say he was *tired*." She grimaced. "Goodbye, Mr. Clevenger. I hope you have a good night's rest. I'll expect you in Brandon with lots of information."

I said, "You're cute when you're mad, but you're prettier when you laugh."

She looked up. After a long pause she said warily, "You can skip the romantic approach. And don't do the little girl any great big favors."

I said, "It's hell what a man will do to avoid having to sleep in a leaky tent in the rain, isn't it?"

She smiled slowly. Her smile was as good as her laugh, kind of pert and young and impudent. "And it's hell what a girl will do to keep from having to sleep alone, isn't it?"

5

When I came out of the bathroom, dressed, she was standing at the gray window looking at the street four stories below. She made a rather intriguing picture there, in the pale dawn light, since she was wearing only the white silk shirt that, somehow, we'd never got around to taking off her. It had been an impromptu come-as-you-are kind of performance, as love scenes go. I couldn't help noting, as I crossed the room, that the improvised nightshirt wasn't quite as long as it would have been, had it been designed for a sleeping garment in the first place.

"Well, I'll get in touch with you in Brandon," I said, businesslike. I wasn't quite sure what our relationship was supposed to be now.

Elaine turned from the window to face me. After a moment she drew the rumpled shirt together in front and started to button it, more from a sense of tidiness, I gathered, than from any real feeling of modesty. There was, after all, no further reason for us to be modest with each other. She gave me a funny, wry smile.

"I suppose you think I'm a cheap little tramp," she said.

I said, "A man can't win around here. If he doesn't sleep with you, he's taking a slap at your appearance, and if he does, he's maligning your character."

I half expected her to be angry, but she just grinned. Then she stopped grinning and said, "It's a lousy business, darling. I suppose you know what I'll do the minute you're out of the room. I'll take the glass you drank out of and send it in to have the fingerprints checked."

I laughed. "Well, I'm glad you said that. I was just trying to work up a plausible excuse for walking off with that bottle of Scotch you were pouring out of, so I could see what I could develop on it with my do-it-yourself detective kit. My boss has a few Washington connections that might be able to run down your prints for us."

"Not unless I wanted them run down," she said, smiling. "But help yourself. I think Mike Green already got a set, much more subtly, but I don't mind if you take one, too. Just don't let the liquor go to waste. That would be a crime." She watched me as I found a narrow paper bag in the nearby wastebasket, smoothed it out, and slipped the bottle inside. "Dave."

"Yes."

She was serious again. "What happens in bed never makes any difference. Not in my line of work. I hope you understand that."

"What are you trying to say?"

"Whether I like you or not has nothing to do with anything. If you're not a private detective from Denver, darling, please get in your little car and start driving very fast, any direction. Otherwise there'll be nothing but a small wet spot on the pavement, marked Clevenger."

I said, "It isn't nice of you to keep trying to scare me to death."

She shook her head quickly. "No, don't joke about it. This is big, darling, very big. If you're playing any tricks, you'll be squashed, and I'll help squash you. That's what I'm trying to say. And even if you are a private detective from Denver, and even if you have a very respectable principle and an excellent reason for hanging around, I'd still advise you to go home and work on some nice lucrative divorce case. Because if you get in the way we'll run over you like a steamroller. This woman has got hold of something that… well, it's terribly important. We have to get it back before it's compromised further. There's really no room for any private interests here."

She was very grave and, with her tousled black hair and abbreviated shirt, very cute. I said, "You sound practically subversive, doll. Big government has taken over, and there's no room for the lousy little private dick to make a few lousy little private bucks. Hell, that's dictatorship, that's communism. I'll speak to my senator." I reached out and tipped her face up and bent over to kiss her lightly on the mouth, saying: "See you in Brandon."

It was meant to be just a debonair parting gesture from a somewhat older man to a somewhat younger girl—let's not go into the exact age difference involved—but it went wrong. I don't mean that it developed into a passionate, clinging clinch, with breathless declarations of undying love. We weren't the breathless, clinging type. Watching us, you probably wouldn't have known anything had happened at all. And maybe it didn't happen then; maybe it had already happened while we made love and slept for a couple hours close together in the big hotel bed. Maybe we were just becoming aware of it now. But there was no mistaking it.

As a kiss, however, it lasted only a fraction of a second longer than the easy goodbye peck it had been intended to be. Separating, we looked at each other for a moment. I reached up and touched her mop of black hair.

"Elaine the fair," I said. "Elaine the lily maid of Astolat. Tennyson?"

"I think so," she said. "It isn't nice to make fun of me."

"You were kind of casual about letting me in here," I said. "Better start being careful with doors, lily maid, like Mike wasn't."

She grinned. "What can acid do to me that hasn't already been done?"

"At least you've still got a face, repulsive though it may be," I said. "We know a guy who hasn't."

Elaine drew a long breath, and said, "The Moosehead Lodge. Room 14."

"Sure," I said and went out without looking back. Walking down the hall to the elevator, I wanted to sock the wall with my fist—or with my head, to knock some sense into it. It was such an unnecessary damn complication. I mean, the girl wasn't even particularly goodlooking.

Anyway, there was no place here, I told myself sternly, for emotional involvement. I'd lied to her already, several times, and I was under orders to lie again and keep on lying—Mac had been quite specific on the point that other agencies could not be informed. And I wasn't even sure that Elaine hadn't lied to me, in return, or at least withheld part of the truth—a rather unpleasant part of the truth, that I was bound to investigate if I was going to do my job right. Everything would have been much simpler if I could have maintained an objective viewpoint. Well, that's what I got for going to bed with people for the wrong reasons.

Outside, it was a bleak morning with low, gray clouds. Sitting in the Volkswagen, I glanced through the newspaper I'd picked up in the hotel lobby, to bring myself up to date and also, I guess, to settle my thoughts before I got on the phone and made official conversation.

Newswise, it had been a frantic twenty-four hours, I gathered, that I'd spent on the road and in bed. South of the border, in the U.S.A., a jet airliner had blown up in midair, the Air Force had misplaced a bomber on a training mission, the Navy had announced an atomic sub missing and presumed lost, and two ships had collided in some harbor. Still farther south, in Mexico, a bus had fallen off a mountain. The international political scene was as loused-up as ever. I couldn't see that any of this was related to my mission, but it was a little early to tell, since I still didn't know exactly what my mission was.

Up here in Canada, things had been only a little quieter. A bush pilot was down in the brush somewhere to the north. A dynamite bomb had exploded in Montreal, in the province of Quebec, leading to speculations as to whether the French-speaking liberation movement was embarking on a new wave of terrorism. And closer to home—well, to the borrowed car in which I sat, that was as much home as I had—the penitentiary at Brandon had lost a couple of prisoners.

I frowned at the last item thoughtfully. It was definitely related to my mission, since it meant that the highways would probably be full of Canadian cops of all kinds, looking for the escaped convicts. I hoped they'd find them fast. Whatever it was I was supposed to do up here, I'd do it a lot easier without the local law looking over my shoulder.

There was a brief mention of a dead man found in a Regina motel—a United States citizen identified as Michael Green, of Napa, California. It was stated that, although death had apparently been caused by a self-administered overdose of sedative, the authorities were not quite satisfied with certain features of the case, and the investigation was being continued.

Nobody seemed to be interested in me sitting there. I drove off. Nobody seemed to be following me. I found a phone booth at the corner of a filling station that handled a brand of gasoline I'd never heard of before—White Rose, if it matters—and I stood inside the booth watching rain drip off the black VW while I talked.

"Say five-two, sir," I said. "Maybe a hundred and ten.

Maybe twenty-five. Hair black. Eyes gray. Appendix scar. Small, crooked scar on right thigh that could have come from an old compound fracture. Maybe she fell out of a tree or something when she was a kid. She looks as if she'd have been the tree-climbing type." I knew there was something I'd forgotten. The funny thing was, I had to think a moment to remember it. "Oh, yes. She apparently had smallpox as a kid. It shows on her face."

Mac said dryly, two thousand miles away, "You seem to have made a thorough investigation, Eric. It wasn't really necessary. We have already checked on Miss Harms at Greg's request. She is perfectly genuine."

"Sure," I said. "Well, I couldn't take her word for it I've got some fingerprints on a bottle, but under the circumstances I guess I'll just forget about what's outside and concentrate on what's inside, which happens to be pretty good Scotch. I see you got hold of your discreet official, sir. There is an announcement in the paper, but it doesn't say much. Did you happen to think to give them a dental description? I mean, there wasn't much in the way of a face or fingerprints to go by, and there's always a possibility that somebody's being very, very clever."

Mac said, "The possibility occurred to me, also. Gregory's identification is positive. We can dismiss the melodramatic idea of a substitution. With regard to this girl, we can check out the fingerprints you have, if you feel it's necessary."

I hesitated. "No," I said. "I think she's genuine, all right. But—"

"What is it that disturbs you, Eric? I gather you're not entirely satisfied."

I told myself not to be a sentimental dope. I was a coldblooded government agent on coldblooded government business, and no damn female could deflect me from my duty by a single degree.

"I don't like that acid, sir," I said. "Isn't it kind of out of character, for the subject we're watching? I mean, the Drilling subject."

Mac was silent for a moment, far away. Then he said slowly, "It seems to be a simple variation of the old ammonia technique. Silent and effective. If you first blind a man with a reagent that also causes excruciating, disabling pain, you can then deal with him at your leisure."

"Sure," I said. "But there are a couple of questions that bother me. Like, how would Mrs. Genevieve Drilling, housewife, learn about the old ammonia technique? And where would she get the drug—whatever it was, and however it was administered—that finished Greg off? I don't think the acid killed him."

Mac said, "It didn't. The cause of death was cyanide or some derivative, but we don't yet know exactly how it was administered. That angle is still under investigation. It could have been done with a dart fired from an air gun or spring gun, the kind that's often camouflaged as a man's cigarette case or a woman's compact. Or it could have been done quite simply with a hypodermic, if the murderer wanted to risk working in that close."

"I know," I said. "But now you're talking about real

tricky spy stuff, sir. I didn't know we were dealing with a pro."

"Mrs. Drilling isn't a professional, but her male friend is."

"And just where is this guy Ruyter supposed to be hanging out with his ready stock of acids and poisons? Have we any reason to believe he's here in Regina?"

"We have no evidence that he isn't," Mac said. "At the moment we do not know, unfortunately, just where Mr. Ruyter is. Of course, if he should be in Regina, he could have committed the murder himself."

"It's a possibility," I said. "There's another possibility, sir, that I think we'd better consider."

"Go on."

I looked at the black Volkswagen in the rain, and I thought of a girl in black pants and a white shirt, and I thought of a girl in just a white shirt.

I said, "You said it was a variation of the old ammonia technique. But there's one big difference. The ammonia treatment generally wears off in time. As a rule it's employed by people who don't want to inflict permanent damage. But we've got a sadistic screwball loose here, somebody who likes to torment his, or her, victims before killing them." I hesitated, and went on stiffly: "Either that or we've got somebody with a real big personal hate, say a girl with a marred face who's had a goodlooking man turn her down crushingly, with snide remarks about her disfigurement."

6

Having said it, I felt much better. As Elaine herself had said, what happens in bed never makes any difference; and I'd done my duty, I'd made my report. Nobody, not even I, could accuse me of concealing my suspicions because I happened to like the girl.

After a pause, Mac spoke in the phone: "You're referring to Miss Harms, I presume. Are you proposing this theory seriously, Eric?"

"No, just calling attention to it as a possibility, sir. I thought I'd better mention it before we got our Drilling thinking all mixed up with a murder that might have been committed by somebody else."

"What kind of evidence do you have?"

"Strictly circumstantial. Motive and opportunity—she admits she was at the motel. She says Greg was already dead when she got there, but we don't have to believe her. And the weapon would have posed no problem for a trained agent, nor would finding the guts to use it."

THE RAVAGERS 47

There was another, longer silence. Then Mac said, "You realize that we are not assigned to investigate a homicide, Eric. That is a problem for the local police, and for the girl's own department, if she's guilty."

It was what I'd hoped he'd say. We don't make a fetish of avenging our dead; half the time we don't even stick around to bury them.

"Yes, sir," I said.

"Any other problems?"

"Yes, sir. There are two male characters snooping around. One is tall, either bald or very blond—I couldn't really make him out in the dark—and answers to the name of Larry. He tends to get lost in the woods at night."

Mac said, "Larry Fenton. The other goes by the name of Marcus Johnston. He is the senior of the pair, in charge. I do not think he gets lost in the woods. A good, experienced man, apparently. This information came from the same source as that about Miss Harms. Whether they are all working together, or she is operating independently, I could not determine. I did not wish to ask too many questions. It is a rather delicate situation."

I waited for him to elaborate, but he didn't, so I said, "And then there's this guy Ruyter, whatever his real name may be. If we don't know where he is now, do we at least have some notion of where and when Mrs. Drilling is expecting to make contact with him?"

"That contact may already have been made, once."

"How's that, sir?"

"There are about twenty-four hours of her time

unaccounted for since she left White Falls."

"Only twenty-four?" I said. "Elaine Harms said three days."

"What Miss Harms' department can account for, and what we can account for, are two different things, Eric."

"Yes, sir," I said, chastened. "I'm beginning to gather that, sir. Like you said, a delicate situation, sir."

"Mrs. Drilling was carefully escorted on her way, for reasons that will become clear to you. The surveillance was intended to be complete and, of course, undetected, at least in the initial stages: she was supposed to think she'd got away from White Falls unobserved. Unfortunately for the completeness, modern cars are built very low, for what purpose I have never discovered, except to knock off your hat as you get in. The man who was keeping an eye on the subject in British Columbia—not one of ours—was driving one of these rakish objects of the automotive designer's art. Mrs. Drilling, as you know, drives a half-ton pickup truck. You can probably guess what happened."

I said, "At a certain point the lady headed out into the boondocks and separated the men from the boys? Or shall we say, the vehicles from the toys?"

"Precisely. She and the little girl went fishing at a mountain lake. Whether by accident or design, they picked a lake, the road to which was atrocious. The truck, with adequate clearance, had no real trouble, but the streamlined sedan quickly came to a halt with a punctured oil pan and other damage. Mother and daughter had brought sleeping bags. They spent the night at the lake, while the agent who was supposed to watch them was busy walking out to find a wrecker. Next day they came back to the trailer, which they had left below, conspicuously displaying a handsome mess of rainbow trout."

"So our girl's a fisherwoman," I said.

Mac said, "Or somebody is. What she encountered up there besides fish remains unknown. The agent with the stylish taste in automobiles was withdrawn after he'd pointed out the right camp to Greg, who took over the job of surveillance a little earlier than had been planned."

I said, "Correct me if I'm wrong, sir, but I'm gradually getting the impression this is a putup job. If they'd been following her clear from the state of Washington, with just the one slip, they could presumably have stopped her and retrieved the precious documents at any time."

"Any time after the first six hours, approximately." I heard papers rustle a couple of thousand miles away. "According to the report I have here, at three-twenty P.M. of the day she left home Mrs. Drilling stopped in a small town and mailed a well-filled manila envelope to a Mrs. Ann Oberon, General Delivery, Inverness, Cape Breton Isle, Nova Scotia. Inverness is a mining town on the Atlantic coast—an ex-mining town, I should say, since the local coal mines have been shut down for years. Mrs. Drilling's middle name is Ann, and her maiden name was O'Brien. The transition from O'Brien to Oberon has been made before."

I said, "Like the one from Smith to Smythe. Or O'Leary to Alire, down Mexico way. Elaine Harms said she was proceeding on the theory that the lady might have mailed the stuff to herself somewhere, but she didn't seem certain and she didn't seem to know where."

"I have already indicated that Miss Harms' agency has been permitted to know only as much as is considered good for them."

"I see," I said. "So it's definitely a plant. And they're not in on it, but we are."

"Precisely."

"What about the Drilling woman? Does she know the papers are phony?"

"Of course not. Mrs. Drilling's undisciplined, romantic impulses are being harnessed, like the power of the atom, for patriotic purposes. It was known when Ruyter appeared in this country last fall that his mission was to obtain information about Dr. Drilling's work at White Falls. When it became apparent that he was planning to get his information through the wife, the affair was watched with great interest and careful plans were laid to take advantage of it. There was a setback last winter when somebody less susceptible to his charms called the F.B.I. anonymously and suggested that Hans Ruyter's credentials should be investigated. It could have been a test to see how we—well, the agency then conducting the operation—would react. It could not be ignored. Ruyter was therefore banished in a convincing manner, but it was hoped that he would eventually get in touch with Mrs.

Drilling, his last chance of accomplishing his assignment, and he did. When his summons came, she responded eagerly, according to the report. The prepared papers were made available to her, with Dr. Drilling's assistance, and she took them."

I said, "So the husband helped set her up. Nice guy."

"I gather that Dr. Drilling feels that his honor has been besmirched and his reputation tarnished by his young wife's shameless and treasonable behavior."

"He sounds like a stuffed shirt," I said.

"He is one," Mac said. "But let us not complain, since his character operates in our favor. He has cooperated fully to date, and he has promised to give us any further help we may need."

"Good," I said. "I have an idea for a possible approach to the wife and child, but he's going to have to back me up, if somebody should check."

"He will," Mac said. "Tell me what he is to say and he will say it. In addition to his other motives, he fears for his career. To continue with the story, after leaving White Falls, Mrs. Drilling proceeded to drive north. The briefcase she disposed of almost immediately, in a trash burner in a roadside picnic area, making an attempt, not entirely successful, to destroy it by fire. Later the same day she mailed the envelope, as I have said. An agent managed to catch a glimpse of the address without resorting to official means that might have betrayed our interest should anyone inquire later. Naturally, the one thing that must not cross Mrs. Drilling's mind, or the minds of Ruyter and whatever associates he may have, is that we *want* those papers to go through."

I frowned at the rain on the glass of the booth. "Objection, sir. Anybody can stuff an envelope full of paper and put it in the mail. There's such a thing as a decoy, sir. It would have been more reassuring if the guy had looked inside."

"The risks involved in tampering with the envelope were too great. The next best thing was done instead. The woman was, of course, expecting to be traced eventually, stopped, questioned, and searched. Presumably that was why she had disposed of the incriminating evidence at the earliest possible moment. It was arranged for her expectations to be fulfilled shortly after she entered Canada, and it was definitely established that she no longer had any valuable documents in her possession."

"I see. Elaine said the outfit had been searched. This was before they lost track of her for a day."

"Yes."

"So she had the stuff when she left White Falls and she didn't have it when she got to B.C. And she mailed only one item, I suppose, on the way."

Mac said, "That is how it stands. It is not absolutely watertight, of course, but the agency from which we are taking over feels certain that she is heading for Inverness and that the material will be awaiting her there."

I said, "And we want those papers to go through, you say?"

"Of course. As far as we are concerned, that is the

whole purpose of the operation. We are to see that she is successful in retrieving the material in Inverness and making delivery."

"Why? Have the scientific boys at White Falls cooked up something nice and misleading that they want served up with authentic trimmings to throw the other side's research off the tracks?"

Mac said, "The reasons for the instructions have not been confided to us, Eric."

I grinned at the dry tone of his voice. "I dig you, sir. It's a big cake and we get to cut only a small slice off it. Ours not to reason why, and all that jazz. Back to that mountain lake our predecessor couldn't make in his Detroit chariot. If Mrs. Drilling did meet Ruyter there for a council of war, would you say they've probably set up another rendezvous farther east?"

"It seems likely. One or more. Perhaps he will travel clear to the Atlantic coast independently and wait for her there. But perhaps not. She is, after all, an amateur; he may not trust her to make it alone. He may hover nearby, ready with secret advice and encouragement."

I said, "And if I should chance to bump into him, what do I do, sir? Bow and excuse myself politely?"

"Naturally. He must not be harmed."

I said, "Hell, can't I even drown the kid if I feel aggressive? I mean, does this whole damn caravan have to get through intact? And are you sure there isn't a dog or cat or pet parakeet I'm supposed to look out for, too?" He did not respond to my sarcasm. I sighed. "Yes, sir.

Mrs. Drilling and entourage are to get where they want to go with any documents they care to bring along. Now tell me, sir, what's apt to get in their way that's so tough we've been called in for escort duty."

Mac said, sounding surprised and rather reproachful, "You're not thinking, Eric."

"What am I not thinking of?"

"Consider," he said, "that as far as all but a very few people in the world know, this woman has stolen highly secret information endangering the U.S. national security. This has, of course, been reported through all the usual channels—after as much delay as was considered safe, to give her the best start possible—and all the usual organizations are now taking all the usual actions. Well, you have already encountered three typical representatives. There may be more. Naturally we cannot request the withdrawal of agents assigned to the Drilling case by other departments. If there should be a leak, it would let our opponents know that we're not quite as eager to repossess Dr. Drilling's stolen notes as we're pretending to be. Do you understand?"

"I'm beginning to catch on. The lost-document drill must be carried out to the last detail, or somebody might begin to question the authenticity of the missing, priceless scientific material."

"Precisely. And still, Mrs. Drilling and Ruyter *must* get through. Not only must they get through, they must be free and clear at the critical moment, after the papers have been retrieved from the Inverness Post Office. They must get away clean by whatever route Ruyter chooses to leave the country. It is your job to arrange this after doing something very convincing to persuade them that you have no patriotic motives or connections whatever."

"Yeah, convincing," I said sourly. "Like blowing up the Washington Monument, or something. One question."

"Yes, Eric?"

"Joking aside, if things get rough, just how far *do* I go to achieve all this?"

"As far as necessary," he said calmly, two thousand miles away.

I started to speak quickly, and stopped. He would have thought of all the possibilities himself, before handing me the blank check with his signature on it. I didn't have to point out that with such instructions I could easily wind up knee deep in dead men of two nationalities—and dead women, too.

"Yes, sir," I said bitterly. "As far as necessary, sir. Very good, sir. Now with regard to the cover story I've been using, I'm making a few minor changes I hope will meet with your approval…"

7

Sitting in the Volkswagen parked beside the wet campground road, not far from the silver trailer in space twenty-three, I had plenty of time to review the conversation, memorize the description of Hans Ruyter I'd been given, and work out the final details of the story I was about to spring on the Drilling duo, mother and daughter. Then I saw the kid coming through the rain. She was about what I'd expected from the advance publicity. The bare knees were perhaps not quite as knobby as I'd feared they would be, but to make up for it the brown hair was rolled up on those big cylindrical curlers that have practically replaced hats for street wear. I suppose it's stuffy and old fashioned of me to feel that a girl with her hair pinned up belongs at home, but as far as I'm concerned, she can even stay out of the living room if there's company in the house.

The headful of parallel cylinders made Penelope Drilling look like a top-heavy little robot ready to tune in on messages from outer space. Covering the electronic receiving apparatus was a kind of nightcap of transparent plastic to keep the rain off, rigged to tie under the chin. There was a tiny kid face with big stary eyes behind horn-rimmed glasses. The mouth, clumsily lipsticked, looked a little strained from closing over the metal that would eventually give her nice straight teeth, just as the stuff on her head would eventually give her nice curly hair. Atom bombs or no, she obviously had a lot of faith in the future, this kid. She was willing to forever look like hell today so she could look swell tomorrow.

She was wearing a rather short yellow raincoat and yellow rubber boots. She'd been over to the camp laundry—I'd seen her go before I moved into position—and she had a bundle of clothes in her arms. She came splashing along the road at a coltish run, hurrying to get out of the rain, and pulled up, startled, when I stepped out of the Volks in front of her.

"Miss Drilling?" I said.

She eyed me suspiciously and asked, "What do you want?" She started to sidle around me so she'd have a straight run for the trailer if I tried to bite her.

I said, "If you're Penelope Drilling, I have a message for you."

"I can't talk to you," she said, with a glance toward the trailer. Then she asked quickly, "A message? Who's it from?"

"Your father."

"Daddy? What does he—"

"Penny!"

That was a woman's voice, from the trailer door. I suppose I should have felt very clever. I'd carefully picked a spot where Mrs. Drilling could see me accosting her daughter if she just glanced out the window. She'd reacted as I'd hoped, but I felt kind of disgusted with the whole business. Why hadn't the damn woman left her child out of it, if she had to go playing secret games with secret men and secret documents? And come to that, why hadn't I figured out an approach that didn't involve telling lies to a fifteen-year-old kid? I had no messages for her from anybody.

The girl gave me a glance and a kind of shrug. She ran off, hugging her armload of laundry. I hurried after her and got there as, having shooed her daughter inside, Genevieve Drilling was struggling to close the double door of the trailer—they put the screen door inside so it won't get beat up while driving, and it occasionally makes for a little awkwardness.

"Mrs. Drilling?" I said.

She started to open the screen to retrieve the outer door, which had failed to catch, but thought better of it. "All right," she said wearily. "All right, what do *you* want? As if I didn't know!"

"May I come in?"

"I see no reason why you should."

"It's wet out here," I said. I couldn't really see her through the shiny aluminum screen, just a feminine silhouette in a long-skirted garment that looked familiar.

"Why don't you give Penny a break, Mrs. Drilling?" I asked, going into my act. "You're grown up. What you do with your life is your business. But what's in it for her?"

There was a brief pause. "You do that very well," the woman said from the other side of the screen. "The little sob you get into your voice is particularly good. You make it sound just as if you really loved children."

I took a long chance and said, "Actually, I hate the little creeps, Mrs. Drilling, but I have a job to do."

She was silent behind the wire mesh, and I decided I'd fluffed it. The earnest, humorless approach would have been better. Then I heard a reluctant laugh and the screen door swung open. I got no real invitation, but she moved aside when I put my foot on the folding metal step, and she closed both doors behind me when I had entered the trailer.

It was a compact little portable house with a double bed set crosswise at one end, facing a sort of dinette at the other, which could presumably also be converted to sleeping purposes. A counter to starboard, with stove and sink and associated cupboards, was balanced by a closet, butane space heater, and john to port. All the comforts of home were there, packed about as tightly as could be managed. The floor was a narrow trail of linoleum through the forest of birch plywood.

The kid, Penny, was sitting on the bed at the far end, wiping rain from her glasses. Without them, her small face had an innocent, vulnerable look. Once the dental remodeling was completed, I decided, she might grow into a reasonably pretty girl. She'd shed her raincoat, which left her dressed in a white shirt and one of the little divided skirts popular that year, that looked like the riding skirt of a movie cowgirl, sawed off above the knees. Neither skirt nor shirt was particularly fresh-looking, but then she was camping out after a fashion, and fifteen is young for sartorial perfection.

I said to her, "I didn't mean to imply that you're a creep, honey. I just had to say something to shake your ma up a bit." Penny gave me a shy glance and showed me a flash of stainless steel in a wary, meaningless smile. Having mended my fences there, I hoped, I turned at last to look at the woman.

It was kind of a shock. I mean, the buildup had been terrific. This was the woman who'd betrayed her husband with a man of unsavory political associations, who'd stolen for him documents, as she thought, of national importance, and who—it was still perfectly possible—might well have sloshed concentrated sulfuric acid into another man's face and, when he was helpless, killed him. It was only natural to expect a pretty far-out female, either an unpredictable featherweight neurotic or a dark figure of mystery and evil—something on the order of a vampire lady with slanting eyes and a sinister smile.

Instead there was just a tallish, nicely proportioned, healthy-looking, pretty woman with, so help me, freckles. I mean, real, all-over freckles, not just a faint, fashionable dusting across the bridge of the nose. Her hair was dark brown with reddish glints, and her face... well, I've already said she was pretty. This is considered a crime in some quarters, where a woman is either beautiful or she's nothing.

Genevieve Drilling wasn't beautiful. You didn't want to hang her on a wall and admire her as a work of art. She was just a damn pretty woman, and you wanted to say something to make her smile, for a start. Once you got her smiling at you, other ideas would doubtless occur to you unless, of course, your heart was set on a vision of pure and perfect loveliness—or unless you were, as I was supposed to be, a dedicated agent whose single-minded devotion to duty was impervious to temptations of any kind.

Well, I didn't have her smiling at me yet, far from it. She was watching me with cool dislike.

"Who are you?" she asked.

"David P. Clevenger, ma'am," I said. "The P stands for Prescott, but I don't use it much."

"Indeed?" she said. "That's very interesting. What do you do, Mr. Prescott Clevenger? To be specific, what are you doing here? Besides molesting young girls, I mean."

I glanced around. "I didn't lest a single mo, did I, honey? All I did was tell you I had a message from your pa. Isn't that right?"

The kid on the bed didn't say anything. She just put her glasses back on her small nose so she could see me clearly. Genevieve Drilling said, "We're not interested in messages from my husband."

I said, "I hear you say it, ma'am. I don't hear her."

The woman's gray-green eyes narrowed. "You sound as if you thought I was intimidating… Penny's here of her own free will, aren't you, darling? She's made her choice. You can tell my husband that."

I said, "I can remember some choices I made in my teens, that I'm damn glad now were overruled by higher authority."

Genevieve Drilling said, "Penny and I understand each other. You go right ahead and deliver my husband's message, Mr. Clevenger, if it will reassure you. I'm surprised he'd allow himself to be distracted from his work long enough to send one, I really am. Both Penny and I were under the distinct impression he'd forgotten that we existed. Well, what does he want?"

"He wants her," I said.

I was aware of the kid stirring slightly behind me. I didn't look that way. I had no idea what Dr. Herbert Drilling really wanted. Maybe children, even his own, just bored him. He sounded as if he might be that kind of a man.

"Just her?" Genevieve said challengingly. "Not me?"

"Nothing was said about you, ma'am."

"Well, that figures," she said dryly. "He always did consider me the only mistake of an otherwise perfectly planned life. Is that all he wants?"

I glanced at her innocently. "Probably not, ma'am, but that's all of his wants I'm concerned with. I gather the U.S. government is attending to some other desires of Dr. Drilling's. That part of it is out of my jurisdiction."

She was watching me closely. "Then you do not represent the U.S. government, Mr. Clevenger?"

"Not me," I said. "I'm a private investigator from Denver, Colorado. We were recommended to your husband by another firm that already had an operative on the job."

She frowned. "You mean the man who calls himself Michael Green? I thought…" She checked herself and was silent.

I said, "That's the man. Mike Green."

She asked, "Why would Mr. Green's detective agency, if that's what he really worked for, recommend a rival firm? Don't tell me the confident, handsome Mr. Green needs help to do a simple job like deceiving a woman?"

I said, "Mike needs plenty of help, ma'am, but none of it's going to do him much good. He's dead. He was murdered last night."

I heard the kid behind me gasp. The woman before me changed expression, started to speak, and stopped. At last she said flatly, "I don't believe you! Murdered?"

"It's in the papers," I said. "Of course they don't say murder. They say suicide." I glanced around. "Duck out to my car and get the newspaper from the back seat, will you, honey?"

"You stay right there, Penny!" snapped her mother. She licked her lips. "The paper says suicide but you say murder, Mr. Clevenger?"

I said, "Mike would never have killed himself, ma'am. What, deprive all the women of the world of his fascinating personality? He'd never have been so cruel."

A faint smile touched the woman's lips briefly. "At least you're telling the truth in one respect. Obviously you did know Mr. Green." She hesitated. "Does anybody… is it known who killed him?"

"I wouldn't know, ma'am. I just read the papers. The police may have their own theories, but as a private op I prefer not to consult with them when I don't have to."

"And why are you telling me this?"

I said, "Hell, you asked me. Excuse me. Didn't mean to swear in front of ladies. But you asked me why I was here. I'm taking Mike's place."

"I see."

"Mike was trying to be subtle, I guess, pretending to be an insurance man on vacation or something. Well, I'm not the subtle type of guy, ma'am. Cards on the table, that's me."

"And you have come about Penny? And that was what Mr. Green was after all the time? I wondered what he had in mind."

I said, "Yes, ma'am. Dr. Drilling would have come himself, I'm told, but apparently the government isn't encouraging him to take any long trips right now, particularly out of the country, so he had to hire somebody to come for him."

I kept looking straight ahead as I said it, ignoring the girl behind me. No matter which parent she preferred, she'd presumably like to think the other cared enough to come after her. It was easier to lie without looking at her face.

Genevieve Drilling laughed abruptly. "You don't mean they suspect he might be in collusion with me? Oh, that's wonderful! That must make him absolutely livid!" She stopped laughing and drew a deep breath. "I'm sorry. I just… Living with that stuffed scientific jackass for over a dozen years, being given a lecture on security every time I asked a simple wifely question… I hope they take away his clearance! That would hurt him worse than… than being castrated, or something. Oh, much worse! After all, he hardly ever…" She stopped, and turned pink, and glanced at her daughter, and at me. "Damn you! How did we get on that?"

It was an interesting glimpse into the Drilling family relationships. I waited, hoping for more, but it didn't come. I said, "You're not going to make it, Mrs. Drilling. I haven't been told what all the big deal is you've got yourself into here, but everybody's got you spotted and you'll never get away. Sooner or later you'll make a wrong move and get clobbered. Do you want Penny to be there when it happens?"

Genevieve was looking at me hard. "I'm surprised, if my husband did hire you, that he didn't ask you, or Mr. Green, to take her back by force."

I said, "You've been seeing too many TV shows, ma'am. No real-life detective agency is going to get involved in a kidnaping, or in anything that could possibly kick back as a kidnaping."

"Then what are you going to do?"

I said, "First off, I'm going to ask you nicely to send

her back, like I'm doing now. Let her go, ma'am. Tell her to pack her stuff and come with me. I'll take good care of her, I promise. I'll have her home by tomorrow night."

"And if I refuse?" Her voice was hard.

I said, "I'm driving a black Volkswagen with Colorado plates. I've got a light green explorer tent—that's the little A-shaped job, not the big umbrella type. Any time you want to talk to me again, either of you, I'll be around. And when the blowup comes, I'll pick up the pieces as best I can. But I'd rather not wait that long. You hear that, Penny? Any time you want to go home, don't worry about clothes or money or anything, just come on over and we'll be on the road in five minutes. Dave Clevenger. Don't forget the name. Okay?"

There was a little silence. I hoped I hadn't been too persuasive. It would be awkward if they decided to send the kid home with me after all.

Then Penny got up slowly. She had to turn sideways and squeeze a bit to get past me in the narrow space, but she made it, and threw her arms around her mother without saying a word. Genevieve Drilling hugged her tightly and looked at me.

"You see, Mr. Clevenger?"

"I see," I said, heading for the door handle. "Well, you can't win them all. I'll be around."

The Canadian drivers along the road had done their best to help her. There hadn't been one who'd let a Volkswagen pass him without a fight, particularly a Volkswagen with U.S. plates. I hadn't met such an aggressive bunch of wheel-jockeys since the last time I drove in competition on a real track, and the bug was underpowered for playing high-speed traffic-tag. Hence my envious glance at the jazzy little Ford with the big mill up front.

I strolled around the swimming pool in a leisurely manner. Partly it was an act for anyone who might be watching, but partly I guess I was stalling mildly, torn between my personal desire to see Elaine again and my professional knowledge that the minute I did see her I'd have to start lying to her. We were on opposite sides. My job was to get the documents through and hers was to stop them. At least she thought it was, and I was not allowed to tell her she was actually there just to make a tricky plant look plausible. There was also a little question of murder between us, but I wasn't brooding heavily over that. Greg had been no great friend of mine. If his death didn't bother Mac, it didn't bother me. Nevertheless, it was another area of uncertainty and possible conflict.

Nobody seemed to be watching me as I came abreast of Number 14. I was just about to commit myself by turning that way when I saw, out of the corner of my eye, a slight movement of the knob, as if someone inside had been about to open the door but had decided against it upon hearing my footsteps outside. Somewhere in my head the warning lights went up on the control board and the sirens began to scream, figuratively speaking. I reminded myself that I was an agent on a mission, not a schoolboy bringing his girl a bunch of posies.

It could, of course, be Elaine herself preparing to fling open the door and greet me with loving arms, but if so why didn't she do it? I moved on without pausing, to the soft-drink machine in the corner of the patio. It took me a while to find a Canadian dime and a little longer to extract the bottle and pry off the cap. The door to Number 14 remained closed.

I walked back deliberately the way I had come, past Elaine's door, taking an occasional swig of the stuff in the bottle, some local preparation that tasted like a certain cough syrup of my childhood, diluted with carbonated water. Around the next corner was the office, with a big picture window. I went inside and found a magazine rack strategically located nearby. I stood there browsing and drinking my medicated-tasting drink, and presently a man came into view at the big window. He walked past, looking neither right nor left.

He could have been any man from any unit in the motel, of course, except that he fit a description I'd recently memorized. He was about five eleven, about thirty-five, he had dark, wavy hair with a touch of gray at the temples, and he had regular, distinguished-looking features. He also had a neat, narrow, dark mustache that was not part of the description, but mustaches are easy to grow.

When he had gone by, I looked up from the magazine

I'd been pretending to examine and watched him walk out across the general parking lot that served the office and restaurant. If he looked around, he'd see me through the glass, but I knew that if he was Hans Ruyter he wouldn't look around. He was a trained man—not one of their best, Mac had said, but competent—and he knew better than to give himself away by glancing over his shoulder in a furtive manner, particularly if he had something to be furtive about.

He walked straight to a parked car. In keeping with his distinguished appearance it was a distinguished car: a big, tan Mercedes sedan, its dignity only slightly marred by the cute curly fins the German designers had stuck on it in belated imitation of the American practice of a few years back. I made a note of the license, a California number. Well, if you want to blend with the tourists on any highway on the continent, you get yourself a set of California plates. I don't think anybody in that state ever stays home.

I watched him drive away smoothly in his expensive imported car. I didn't try to follow. My own car was two blocks away. Anyway, I didn't think that as Dave Clevenger, private dick, I was supposed to ever recognize Mr. Ruyter, let alone tail him. And as Matt Helm, agent of the U.S. government, I was under strict orders not to interfere with him, quite the contrary. The fact that I was anxious to stay and find out what he'd been up to in Elaine's room had, I hope, no influence on my decision, since it was more or less a private worry.

I forced myself to give the Mercedes plenty of time to get clear, while I bought the magazine I'd been examining, finished my drink, and asked the lady at the desk where she wanted me to dispose of the bottle. She graciously consented to take care of it for me. I went out of the office and walked slowly back to the door I had passed twice before. I don't suppose I really expected an answer to my knock. There had been a certain stiffness in Hans Ruyter's bearing, a desperately strained naturalness, that had said quite clearly that here was a man who expected hell to break loose behind him, and hoped to get far away before it did.

There was no response to my knock and no sound of movement inside the room. I drew a long breath and glanced around casually. Everything was quiet. I reached in my pocket for my wallet and got out the piece of plastic I'd used once before here in Canada, the one masquerading as a credit card. As I shielded the lock with my body, I carefully avoided remembering the last time I'd opened a door in this illegal manner, and what I'd found on the other side. At least I tried.

The lock was easy. The door swung back. I took extra precautions, going in. The fact that one man had left didn't guarantee that the place was safe; and I wasn't carrying my revolver today. It was hidden away in the VW where nobody was likely to find it without dismantling the car. With the highways full of convict-hunting policemen—we'd hit two roadblocks on the way—wearing an undeclared firearm in what was, after all, a foreign country, had been too much of a risk. However, I did have a rather special little knife, and I had it ready as I entered, fast. Nothing happened. I got the door closed and went once more through the routine of checking closet and bathroom. Then I shut the knife and put it away and went over to the bed where she lay.

I won't say I'd been expecting it, but after seeing Ruyter I wasn't really surprised. So there was no excuse for the sick, shocked feeling I experienced, looking down at her. Actually, it was very peaceful. No acid had been used here. There was a small-caliber automatic pistol in her hand, the little .25 that will hardly shoot through a heavy overcoat, and there was a dark spot on her temple, that was all. There were some powderburns—there always are, with a contact wound—and there was a little blood, but nothing like the mess you get with the larger calibers.

She was wearing a dress tonight, perhaps put on for my benefit: a gay summery print that made her small tomboy face look very pale. A pair of high-heeled white pumps stood neatly on the rug beside the bed. Her eyes were closed. Except for the pallor, and the gun and the wound, she could simply have slipped off her shoes and lain down to take a nap. He'd set the scene carefully. A portable typewriter, presumably hers, stood open on the long, glass-topped gizmo along one wall, that served as combination dresser and writing table. The machine had a piece of paper in it, displaying one line of writing: I'M SORRY I MUST HAVE BEEN CRAZY GOODBYE.

Beside the typewriter stood an empty chemical reagent bottle with a glass stopper. The label had been defaced by the potent liquid that had run down it in streaks, but I could still read the words: *Acid Sulfuric, conc., USP.* Beside the bottle lay a small hypodermic syringe containing a residue of drug that, I had no doubt, would check out the same as the stuff that had killed Greg.

I didn't believe it for a minute, of course, but the picture was clear enough for the stupidest policeman: unable to live with her guilt, Elaine had set out all the evidence, typed her farewell note, and shot herself. Well, she was the logical fall guy for Greg's murder, if you had to have a fall guy. I'd suspected her myself.

I went back to the bed. The shock was wearing off. I suppose I should have been feeling grief in its place. Well, when the job was over, I could get drunk and cry in my beer, or whiskey, or gin. Right now I had other things to do, and I took from my pocket the stained white kid glove I'd found in Greg's room and tried it on the right hand. It was much too large, it slipped on and off loosely, which was just as well, since the operation wasn't one I found particularly enjoyable. I looked at the damaged glove, frowning, trying to reconstruct the murder in which it had figured, and the murder in which it had not, and the stages by which one had led to the other.

A plausible sequence of events wasn't hard to imagine, if you dismissed the notion of a frameup and took the glove to be exactly what it seemed: a betraying clue dropped at the scene by the real murderess, call her Genevieve

Drilling for convenience. Afterwards, realizing that she'd left it, Genevieve could have made contact somehow with her accomplice, Ruyter, and explained the spot she was in. He could have agreed to clean up after her, by giving the police a solution of the case so simple and tidy that they'd be glad to overlook the minor discrepancy of a glove that didn't quite fit. In any case, whatever his reasons, he'd obviously come here to tie up the loose ends of one murder by committing another.

Of course, neither Genevieve nor her Hans knew that the police didn't have the missing glove: I had it. Perhaps Elaine would not have died if they'd known that. And perhaps she would not have died if she had not been expecting me and therefore, perhaps, despite my warning, had not been quite as careful about opening the door as she should have been. I grimaced and shoved the glove back into my pocket. You can take the guilt of the whole world on your shoulders any time you want to try, and many people do, but I didn't have time for the sackcloth-and-ashes routine just then.

As I started for the door, the telephone rang. I hesitated, but it seemed useful to know who was calling, so I took out my handkerchief and used it to pick up the instrument on the third ring. A young male voice I'd heard before in some wet woods in the dark, said:

"Elaine? We just got word from Denver on this Clevenger character you're seeing tonight. He seems to be okay, a real, honest-to-God private eye… Elaine? Who's there?"

The decision wasn't hard to make. I could hang up and leave Larry Fenton and Marcus Johnston guessing, but Elaine had obviously told them she was expecting me—which answered one of Mac's questions. All three of them had apparently been working together. Under the circumstances, the remaining two would be bound to come around to question me when they learned what had happened to Elaine. It was better to give an impression of boyish frankness.

I said, "This is the Clevenger character. If you're the Larry character, you'd better get over here. Bring a shovel, you've got something to bury. If you want me afterwards, I'll be out at the campground. If you don't know where, it's time you found out."

"Listen, you stay right where you—"

I put the phone down. I looked at the bed, but there wasn't anybody there to talk to. I mean, sentimentally telling a dead girl goodbye, or dramatically promising to avenge her, is just a way of talking to yourself, and they lock people up for that. Besides, I reflected grimly, I wasn't being paid to wield the sword of retribution. On the contrary, I was under strict orders to help the murderers escape free and clear.

9

The last pink glow of sunset was just fading from the sky when I came out of there. I reached my car without incident, drove away, and stopped at a filling station after a dozen blocks. While the attendant was putting gas into the Volks, I went into the restroom, locked the door, took out the stained white glove and my knife, and cut my private murder clue into small pieces, which I then flushed down the john a few at a time, not wanting to risk clogging the plumbing.

On the assumption that the incriminating glove did belong to Genevieve Drilling—and who else would Hans Ruyter be covering for?—I couldn't take the risk of keeping it around any longer. I could think of no useful purpose it could serve me, either as Dave Clevenger or as Matt Helm, and I couldn't afford to let it serve anybody else, certainly not anybody with a legalistic mind. The last place for Genevieve to be, if I was to carry out my instructions, was in jail. She was my baby, all murderous, acid-throwing five feet seven of her; and Hans Ruyter, the competent girl-killer, was my baby, too. It was my duty, I reminded myself grimly, to see that nobody hurt a hair of their scheming, vicious, good-looking heads.

At the very least, I told myself as I made the water run for the last time, the glove could have involved me in unnecessary complications, should there be somebody waiting when I got back to camp. I stalled long enough on the way to make reasonably sure there would be.

They weren't in sight, of course. I'd got a fairly secluded site toward the rear of the camp, shielded by trees and bushes, and they were playing it cute. I didn't spot Johnston in the dark, but that Larry character would never go hunting with me. He was one of the jerks who can't sit still, in a duck blind or anywhere else. I had him located in the brush before I was even out of the car.

I left the lights on to illuminate the tent until I could get the gasoline lantern going. They waited until I had it burning brightly. They waited until I'd set it safely on the nearby picnic table and switched off the car lights. Then Johnston came out from behind a tree and pointed a gun at me. I raised my hands politely. Larry came out of his hiding place, if you want to call it that, and walked up to me, and hit me.

It wasn't much of a punch, but I let it knock me down, figuring that was the easiest way to end the fight before it started. A smart private op named Clevenger wouldn't mix it with a couple of armed men he knew to be government agents; and I've never seen much point in

hitting a man with a fist, anyway. All it gets you is some
bruised knuckles and a resentful enemy who is probably
not damaged enough to prevent him from getting back
at you later. There's hardly ever any sense in hitting a
man with anything that doesn't make him dead—that is,
if you've got to hit him at all. But nobody'd told Larry
Fenton that. Having knocked me down, he stepped
forward and kicked me.

"You killed her!" he panted. "Damn you, you killed
her!"

The kick was probably more than tough Mr. Clevenger
should stand for. I looked at Johnston, staying well back
with his gun. *A good, experienced man,* Mac had said,
but at first glance he looked unimpressive: a plump little
figure with gold-rimmed glasses. He had thinning brown
hair combed straight back from a soft white face. You'd
never give him a second look in a crowd. He looked as if
he sold shoes or insurance for a living, and went home
nights to watch TV with a plump little wife and a couple
of plump little children.

At second glance, I noted the cold, alert blue eyes
behind the glasses, and the steady hand holding the gun.
I was relieved. This man wouldn't do anything hasty, nor
would he let his erratic and amateurish partner go too far
astray. It was safe to put on a show for him. He wouldn't get
nervous and shoot a hole in me by mistake. I spoke to him
without looking at Larry, standing over me threateningly.

"Pull it off me," I said. "If it kicks me again, I'll cut its
little foot off, so help me."

"Take it easy, Clevenger," Johnston said. "Take it very easy."

I said, "To hell with you," and reached defiantly into my pants pocket. He didn't shoot. I took out my knife and opened it deliberately. Larry started to reach for me, but Johnston waved him back. I said, "I'll cut it off at the ankle, so help me. Just one more kick and he'll be known as Footless Larry. And you, Chubby, stop waving that fool gun around, hear? You fire it off in the middle of a public campground like this and you'll be making explanations to every cop in Canada."

Johnston regarded me unwaveringly. "You talk pretty big for a lousy private cop."

I said, "You act pretty big for a lousy spy, or counter-spy, operating in a foreign country, probably without permission."

"How do you know what we are? And how did you learn that my partner's name is Larry?"

I said, "Hell, you told me the name yourself. Last night in the bushes outside the Drilling trailer, in the rain. He got lost in the dark and you called to him by name, remember?"

The plump little man looked disconcerted. "You were there?"

"I was there," I said. "Unlike some people, I'm real good in the woods, if I do say so myself."

"And how did you learn so much about our business?"

"When I came on the job, I was told the government had an interest in the case. And last night, when the girl was trying to pump me for information in Regina, she told me she worked for Uncle Sam. And when I picked up the phone in her motel room tonight right here in Brandon, your friend here started making a report to her, on me. I figure that puts you all in the same line of work with the same employer. In the detective business we call it deduction." I looked at him hard. "And now I'm getting up, Chubby. Go ahead and fire that thing, if you think Washington will come back you up. I'm sure they'd love an international protest about U.S. undercover creeps shooting up people north of the border."

"Who's going to protest? You, with murder on your hands?"

I didn't answer immediately. I got to my feet. Larry started to close in again, but again a signal from the older man stopped him. I closed the knife and dropped it into my pocket, looking at Marcus Johnston.

"What's this about a murder?"

"My partner has made it pretty plain. We think you killed Elaine."

I said, "Ah, cut it out. Don't give me that old routine. You come at me frothing at the mouth, throwing it at me hard and sudden, hoping you'll catch me off balance and make me spill something. Well, this hombre doesn't spill that easy. So now let's talk sense. The kid killed herself, and we all know it, and we all know why. Was it her gun?" Their silence said yes. I said, "Okay, then, the only question is, are you going to leave it that way or do you have some notion of framing me for it?"

"Why would we do that?" Johnston asked.

I said, "Income tax men, Treasury agents, G-men, guys like you, who knows why you do anything? You might want to whitewash her for the good of the service, as they say. Maybe it's bad publicity to have your people committing murder and suicide for personal reasons. Or you might just want to get me out of your hair."

"It's not a bad idea," he said. "I'll give it some thought."

I said, "It's a lousy idea. You leave the thing lay and you're finished with it. It started in Regina and it ends here in Brandon."

Larry was staring at his partner in an indignant, incredulous way. "Why are you listening to him, Marcus? He killed her. Elaine would never have killed herself, and she wouldn't have killed anybody else the way that was done. She'd never have used acid like that."

I looked at Johnston, and shook my head. "Where'd you find this one, pal? You mean he really believes this crap he's been spouting? I thought he was just putting on an act."

Larry said violently, "You killed her. You were there, we know you were."

"Sure. I killed her. And then I picked up the phone and told you all about it. Smart me."

"Maybe that's the way you were playing it smart." The younger man turned back to his partner. "Who else had the opportunity? We know Mrs. Drilling never went near the motel. I was watching her every minute she was in town."

I said quickly, "But she did go into town?"

"Well, yes, she did drive in to gas up the truck while the girl fixed dinner, but—"

I said, "That's a lot of work, uncoupling the pickup from the trailer, for some gas she could have got along the road in the morning. But you had your eyes on her every minute?" I studied his face. A hint of uneasiness gave me the cue, and I said, "Gas stations have restrooms as a rule. She didn't go in?" The betraying flicker of his eyelids told me I'd scored a hit, and I went on harshly, "She didn't stay in there kind of a long time, maybe? She had no chance to slip away? No, that's right, you said you were watching her every minute. Through the restroom keyhole, maybe?"

I'd been wondering how Genevieve, under constant surveillance, had managed to talk to Ruyter unseen when she needed help, but I had my answer. They'd presumably arranged to meet at a certain time at a certain filling station where the restrooms were side by side around the corner of the building. He could have been waiting in either section with the door locked, until she signaled by knocking a certain way. Or they could have talked through the wall. But I wasn't about to let these men know what I'd been trying to find out. Ruyter was my secret, my fairhaired boy, to be protected and cherished.

I regarded Larry grimly. He was silent, flushing. He was really pretty young for this business, I saw. The bald head fooled you. It was a kind of patchy baldness, and he'd shaved off the remaining hair with some idea of looking like Yul Brynner, maybe, or just making a virtue of necessity. He was pale and thin, and the hairlessness made his head look skull-like and old, but he really wasn't very far into his twenties.

I decided that he must have been sick or badly wounded recently. This was probably his first job since leaving the hospital. I suppose I should have made allowances. Maybe he was a good man who'd been sent into the field again too soon after a terrible experience of some kind, but I couldn't really believe he'd ever been a ball of fire. I judged him as a green trainee who'd got himself clobbered the first or second time out, and who was going to get clobbered again if he wasn't very lucky. I might even have to do the job myself.

"Well," I said dryly, "she's stacked, I'll say that for Madame Drilling. It must have been interesting to watch."

Larry hesitated. "Well, I didn't really *watch*—" He stopped and turned to Johnston quickly. "She couldn't have slipped out, I swear it, Marcus! And the filling station was on the other side of town from Elaine's motel. She couldn't possibly have got there and back... He stopped.

I said, "If she couldn't have got away from you, what difference does it make how far she had to go? The fact is, she could have backdoored you, and you obviously know it, or you wouldn't be talking so fast to cover up."

Johnston said, "Are you trying to fit Mrs. Drilling for the job, Clevenger? I thought you were the man who said it was suicide."

"I still say it. It's Sonny, here, who keeps trying to

make it murder. I'm just pointing out to him that if it is murder, I'm not the only candidate, thanks."

There was some more talk along these lines, getting us nowhere. I didn't convince Larry of my innocence, and Johnston, I soon realized, didn't need convincing. He was just letting Larry test me with the murder gag. Apparently I checked out okay, because at last he had Larry search me perfunctorily, and then he put his gun away. Pretty soon he was telling me how he wanted me to cooperate and what would happen to me if I didn't.

"There's really no place for a private dick in this operation," he said, "but since you're here…"

"Sure," I said. "But you stay away from me, both of you. I've got troubles enough without being seen associating with a couple of government men. If I learn anything, I'll get in touch."

"See that you do. Come on, Larry."

I watched them go off into the darkness. Then I rubbed the bruised side of my jaw and grimaced. Well, I'd managed to keep them off Ruyter's track for the time being. I lit the Coleman stove and put on a frying pan and cooked a little steak I'd picked up in town. It was stringy and tough. After washing up, I walked over to the rich trailer-folks' part of the camp. There were lights in the silver trailer with the state of Washington plates. I knocked on the door.

Presently the girl, Penny, stuck her head out. She was still wired for interstellar communication, but tonight, instead of her plastic nightcap, she was wearing a pink net hood to keep the precious curlers undisturbed.

"I'd like to speak with your mother," I said.

Her small face looked pinched and frightened. She hesitated, and turned jerkily. "It's that man," she said. "That private detective man. He wants to see you, Mummy."

I said, "Tell her it's about a murder."

That brought a space of silence. I heard Genevieve rise and come to the door. The kid disappeared. Genevieve looked down at me from the trailer door. "What about a murder, Mr. Clevenger?"

"Aren't you going to ask me in?"

She started to glance over her shoulder, as if looking for advice, but checked herself. "No, I'm not going to ask you in!" she snapped. "What do you want?"

I regretted having come. Obviously there was someone in the trailer who didn't belong there, and if it was the man I thought, I didn't want to betray his presence to Larry or Johnston, one of whom was probably watching.

I gave a phony sigh of resignation, and said, "All right, ma'am. Ill go away. I just thought you'd like to hear the latest on Mike Green. He was murdered, all right, like I said, and the young lady who did it committed suicide in Brandon this evening. I thought you'd like to know."

The woman above me said stiffly, "I can't think why you'd think so. If there's anything that interests me less than Mr. Green and his sordid death…"

I said, "I know. It's Mr. Clevenger and his sordid life. Good night, ma'am."

As I walked away, I heard the trailer door slam behind

me. Well, I'd given them the good news; they could relax now. With a slight assist from me, they'd got away with two murders. I wondered why Ruyter had been fool enough to come here, if it was Ruyter—and if it was, I hoped he managed to get himself away unseen before morning.

If not, I'd probably have to figure out some cute way of helping him get clear. The next bodyguard assignment I was given, I hoped I'd get to protect somebody I liked, for a change, but it wasn't a great hope. There are plenty of nice, high-principled guys to do the nice assignments. We just get the ones no one else will have.

10

In the morning it was drizzling again. The Drilling outfit broke camp much earlier today, shortly after seven. This might have caught me asleep, or at least breakfastless, if my evening visit to the trailer hadn't prepared me for a possible change in the behavior pattern.

The early start seemed to foreshadow a long day of hard driving, but here again there was a change. Genevieve wasn't her dashing, truck-driving self this morning. Even after we reached the open highway, she poked along cautiously, passing nobody who wasn't next to standing still, making life very easy for me—but I doubted it was my welfare she was thinking of. I noted that she seemed to be alone in the truck cab. Apparently Penny was in the trailer, and I didn't really think the kid was sitting back there by herself.

House trailers are not designed to be occupied in transit; in fact I believe it's illegal in many places to ride in one. Genevieve was driving as if she was afraid somebody might get seasick back there; she was also driving as if she didn't want to take the slightest chance of attracting the attention of a speed cop or becoming involved in an accident.

We were well into the province of Manitoba by now, and the prairie scenery of Saskatchewan was giving way to more rolling country with patches of woods. As we cruised through a stretch of piney forest, Genevieve suddenly pulled out onto the shoulder of the highway and brought her truck and trailer to a halt. I drove past, intending to park beyond the next curve and sneak back for a look, but right around the corner I ran into a police roadblock.

There was nothing to do but act natural and touristy, but as I rolled up to the barricade I couldn't help wondering if Genevieve had stopped because of it, and if so, how she'd known it was there. A tall Mountie with a widebrimmed hat and a yellow cavalry stripe down his pants came up and looked into the Volkswagen with a murmured apology. He straightened up and waved me on, but something was beginning to stir inside my head— call it intelligence if you like—and I didn't drive off right away. Instead I put on a look of busybody curiosity and leaned out the window.

"Are you fellows still looking for those escaped convicts around here?" I asked. "What makes you think they're still hanging around, with all the north woods to escape into? I should think they'd be halfway to Hudson Bay by now."

"One is a local lad, sir," the Mountie said. "We think he may have found somebody to hide him temporarily. At least there's a report that both men were seen in Brandon as late as last night."

"I see," I said. "You mean he's lived around the penitentiary all his life so he knows the routines you're apt to use? That makes it tough, I guess."

"Yes, sir."

I sent the car ahead. The idea that was germinating in my mind was so farfetched that I couldn't take it seriously. Still, something was definitely wrong with Genevieve—she'd behaved oddly both last night and this morning—and until I had a good explanation I couldn't afford to dismiss any possibilities.

I parked the Volkswagen around the next bend, got my binoculars out of the little trunk up front, and returned on foot to a spot among the trees from which I had a view of the roadblock. Presently the blue truck and the silver trailer rolled up to the waiting policeman and stopped obediently. Genevieve was at the wheel of the pickup. I couldn't see anybody in the cab with her.

The tall Mountie who'd inspected me looked in her window and straightened up, satisfied. His partner went back to the trailer and looked inside. Apparently he found nothing amiss, either, for he closed the door and waved Genevieve on. I let her drive past my hiding place without revealing myself, but when I got back to the place where I'd parked my car, she'd pulled off the road behind it. She was sitting in the pickup, hunched over the steering wheel as I'd seen her once before, with her face buried in her hands.

When she became aware of me at the window, she raised her head. She hadn't really been crying, I saw. Her eyes were dry, but they were big and desperate.

I said, in my Clevenger role, "Okay, ma'am, what's going on? Where's the girl? Where's Penny?"

Genevieve just stared at me. Her look was hostile, but it held a hint of speculation, as if she was wondering whether the situation was bad enough to justify taking a gamble on confiding in a creature like me. When she didn't speak at once, I shrugged and went back to the trailer, opened the door cautiously, and climbed inside. It occurred to me that if the woman in the truck should decide to take off, I'd be kidnaped, short of a flying leap to the hard pavement, but I couldn't see what she'd gain by it and neither, apparently, could she. We remained motionless. The trailer was empty. It had a neat, clean look, as if it had just been carefully tidied to hide all traces of the most recent occupant or occupants.

I checked the tiny combination john and shower, and the little plywood closet. The Royal Canadian Mounted Police should have been ashamed of themselves. There were enough teenage clothes around to raise the interesting question of where the owner had got to. I glanced through the various drawers, finding nothing but kitchen stuff, clothes, a wad of comic books and, cached away under the bed, a collection of old playthings that Miss Drilling would probably repudiate now that she was fifteen: everything to keep a kid entertained on a camping trip, from slingshots and water pistols to picture puzzles and pretty little dolls with fancy wardrobes. What I was looking for wasn't exactly clear in my mind, but it seemed a pity to pass up the opportunity.

I made a quick examination of a miniature dresser built into the corner by the bed. Hearing footsteps on the gravel outside, I was just about to shove the last drawer closed when something white caught my eye and I picked it up: a left-handed white kid glove that looked familiar. There was no mate in the drawer. I guess it was what I'd been looking for. I'd recently flushed a similar right-hand glove down a toilet in Brandon. And doubts I might have about its ownership were no longer tenable. It was too big for the kid; it had to belong to the mother.

I dropped the glove back and closed the drawer as Genevieve stepped up to the doorway behind me, causing the trailer to sway on its springs.

"You're hardly likely to find my daughter hiding in there," she said tartly. "If it's Penny you're looking for."

I turned to face her. "Penny," I said, "or a clue to her whereabouts. We detectives are always looking for clues. Where is she, Mrs. Drilling?"

The woman faced me stiffly. "If I told you," she said, "you wouldn't believe me."

"Try me."

"She's out there, somewhere." Genevieve gestured toward the woods visible through the open trailer door. She hesitated briefly, then her words came with a rush: "You're the last man in the world I'd ask for help, but... but I have no choice. If I don't do exactly what they said, they'll kill her. If they even see me talking to you, they'll kill her."

"Who?"

She drew a long breath and said bitterly, "It's absolutely crazy. With… with everything else I've got working against me, I've got to run into a pair of escaped convicts! You can laugh any time, Mr. Clevenger. Laugh, why don't you? It's really very funny, isn't it? Oh, my God!"

It was what I'd begun to suspect, of course, but it wasn't a story a cynical private eye would be likely to buy right off the shelf. I stared at her hard-eyed, therefore, as if offended that she'd try such a silly yarn on me. The funny thing was that finding the glove in her dresser drawer seemed to make me capable of regarding her with greater tolerance than before. Now that I'd tracked down my solitary clue, I could stop thinking like a sleuth. I could remember that murder was really not my business. My job was to gain the confidence of this woman, not put her in the electric chair.

The sunshine striking through the doorway behind her brought out reddish lights in her thick hair. It occurred to me that with the red hair and the freckles and the general conformation of her face and figure—not to mention the maiden name of O'Brien—she was undoubtedly Irish. Well, they're a dark, unpredictable, high-tempered race, I'm told, but for some reason the thought disturbed me. What she was supposed to have done didn't really fit in with my notion of the behavior of a healthy Irish girl of reasonable intelligence and mental stability. Of course, some of the most normal-looking people I've known turned out to be real psychiatric specimens when the pressure came on, and there was no doubt this woman was under heavy pressure.

Still, she looked pretty strong and steady, standing there. She was wearing a dark, full-skirted cotton dress, which was a point in her favor. In my opinion, just about the only valid excuse for feminine pants is a horse or a pair of skis. Her legs were bare and she had on brown sneakers with white rubber soles. She was really a damn goodlooking woman. I couldn't help thinking it was a shame she was probably going to wind up dead or in jail—or in Russia, if that's where they were heading— just because she was a sucker for romance as represented by a slick undercover operator named Ruyter.

When I didn't speak, she said, "I told you you wouldn't believe me."

I said, "It's pretty hard to accept, ma'am. Here you are, a lady on the lam, with an escort of at least two U.S. agents and one private op, and you want me to believe that a couple of cons just happened to pick *your* trailer to hide in? That's a pretty large coincidence."

She shook her head quickly. "Not as large as you'd think, Mr. Clevenger. One of the men, the younger one, had a girlfriend in Brandon who hid them out while they were figuring how to get through the police net. She looked over the trailers in camp and picked ours because it was the only one without a man around. A woman and a young girl alone would be easier to handle, they thought."

I moved my shoulders. "You make it sound real plausible, ma'am. When are these two miscreants supposed to have descended on you?"

She disregarded my cynicism. "They slipped in quite suddenly right after dark, and took me by surprise," she said. "As a matter of fact, when they knocked on the door, I thought it was you or one of those other two government men who've been following me. The next thing I knew, the younger one had a knife in my side." She indicated the place by rubbing it with her elbow. "He was rather rough. I'm not a heroine and… and of course, I had Penny to think of. That was only a few minutes before your visit last night. You can understand why I didn't invite you inside!"

I studied her thoughtfully. "And they spent the night with you? Did they give you a bad time? Or the kid?" Genevieve laughed shortly. "Not the way you probably mean, Mr. Clevenger. Oh, it wasn't fun, but the younger one had already seen his girl, remember, and the older one was just interested in a whiskey bottle I had in the cupboard. *That's* what he'd been missing behind bars."

"Describe them."

"Don't tell me you're beginning to believe me!" Her voice was sharp. "The younger one is about twenty, tall, slim, and goodlooking, if you like punks. I believe that's the term. You know what I mean. I'm sure that in civilian life he had a ducktail haircut, or the Canadian equivalent. He had a big hunting knife his girl had found for him…"

"How big?"

"Oh, about six inches in the blade. He kept brandishing it like Cyrano de Bergerac. He told us proudly that he was a real bad boy with a knife, that's how he'd come to be in prison, for killing a man. The older convict was fifty-five or sixty, a mean little dried up weasel of a man with a terrible thirst. I don't know what crime he'd committed, but I'm sure he's capable of anything that doesn't require courage. He wanted to get another bottle somewhere this morning, but the boy said he'd cut his throat if he tried. They almost had a fight over it. The older one grabbed my big kitchen knife, but it was just a bluff, and he backed down whining. He's still got the knife, though. It's a nasty weapon, Mr. Clevenger, at least ten inches long. I keep it very sharp."

"Two knives," I said. "That's all? No guns?"

"You do believe me now?"

I moved my shoulders. "The question concerned firearms, Mrs. Drilling."

"No firearms. I know because they looked all over the trailer, hoping to find a rifle or pistol." She laughed wryly. "Everybody searches my trailer, from the government on down."

"And they've got your daughter," I said. I looked at a pair of cased spectacles lying on the formica counter, and slid them out of the case, and looked through them, absently. The frames were much too small for me, and the prescription, as far as I could judge, checked with what I'd been told of the kid's eyesight: she was pretty myopic.

Presumably she'd inherited it from her scientific papa, since mama seemed to get along quite well without glasses.

I thought of a small nearsighted girl with braces on her teeth, out in the woods with two criminals, at least one a murderer. I reminded myself that I wasn't here to look after children. On the other hand, my cover story did require me to show a certain concern for Penny's welfare, and it might be a way of improving my relations with the woman facing me.

I said, stalling, "Can she see without these? They're pretty strong."

"It's an old prescription. She has her glasses. She just brought those along for a spare."

"Why did you bring her along, Mrs. Drilling? Why didn't you leave her home where she'd be safe?"

Genevieve's gray-green eyes narrowed. "Safe? Alone in a big house with a father who'd rather watch his tame light rays or whatever they are? I didn't know I was going to run into a prison break, Mr. Clevenger."

I said, "Still, a woman leaving her husband for another man doesn't usually take her offspring with her."

"Oh, you know about Hans." She shrugged. "Doesn't she? Have you made a study of women and the way they leave their husbands? I simply told Hans he'd have to take both of us or neither."

"I don't suppose it's any use asking where you're planning to meet this Hans character."

She said, "No, and why would you care? You're just a private detective hired to take an interest in Penny's welfare. What do you care about Hans, or the scientific formulas I'm supposed to have stolen or any of that? I'm afraid your badge is showing, and it isn't a private badge. Well, you never were very convincing as a detective, and right now I don't care what you are. Just… just help me get Penny back safely, please."

I looked at her grimly. Maybe the question about Hans had been a mistake, but at least I had her asking a favor and saying please.

I said, "You're a stubborn lady, Mrs. Drilling. You're bound to tie me to a government job. Well, let's not waste time on that now. What instructions are these hypothetical convicts supposed to have given you?"

She snapped, "They're not hypothetical, damn you! Do you want me to show you where his knife drew blood?" I didn't say anything, and she went on in a different tone: "I'm supposed to meet them up a road just ahead. The younger one was riding in front with me, lying on the floor. I helped him slip into the cab just before daylight. After we got on the highway, he had me describe the landmarks we passed. He seemed to know there might be a roadblock around the curve back there. He made me pull out, and he got his friend out of the trailer, and Penny. He said for me to go through the police alone, if they were there, and then take the first dirt road to the right and drive to a lake about two miles back from the highway and wait. They'd join me there. If I wasn't there when they arrived, or if I warned the police…" She stopped.

I said, "I know. They'd kill Penny. Presumably with

flourishes. Well, suppose we find this dirt road. You lead, I'll follow in the Volksie. Stop when you're out of sight of the highway."

"What are you going to do?"

"I'll tell you when we have this safari off the highway," I said. "Right now let's get out of sight before one of those policemen sees us and gets curious."

She regarded me for a moment, frowning. I suppose she was wondering just how big a mistake she was making in trusting me. Then she turned and climbed down into the daylight and walked forward to the truck without looking back, leaving me to close the trailer door.

11

I cut a nice, straight little Christmas tree with my camp hatchet. While Genevieve watched, I trimmed off most of the branches, and chopped off the upper part of the trunk that was less than an inch in diameter, as well as the lower part that was greater than an inch and a half. This gave me a tough, serviceable club or nightstick somewhat shorter than three feet and rather sticky with pitch.

I looked regretfully at the hatchet as I slipped the leather sheath back on it and put it away in the car. I've done some tomahawk-type practice in my time, but a man with a couple of pounds of steel tossed into his head or chest is apt to die, and we'd given the Canadian authorities two bodies to worry about already, so I thought it would be well to keep the mayhem to a minimum.

Genevieve was regarding me dubiously. "Haven't you got a gun?" she asked. "I thought all detectives were simply weighted down with firearms till they could barely walk. And all secret agents, too. Whichever you are."

I had no intention of revealing the extent of my armaments unnecessarily. She might decide to use the knowledge against me later.

I said, "You've been watching TV, ma'am. In real life, guns are often more damn trouble than they're worth, particularly in a foreign country with pretty strict import laws. If I did have a pistol here, it would be illegal, and if I were to shoot somebody with it, even an escaped murderer, I'd have a lot of explaining to do." I hefted my club experimentally. "Don't worry about it, ma'am. One good man with a stick can handle half a dozen bad men with knives."

She said dryly, "I always did like modest people. Well, I hope you're as good as you think."

"Remember, one of them is almost sure to have a blade at Penny's throat," I said. "It's the obvious precaution. Wave a firearm at him and he's apt to get nervous. He might even do something hasty. But if I show myself practically unarmed…" I shrugged. "If you have a better idea, let's hear it."

She hesitated. "Well, there's the obvious suggestion. I'm surprised you haven't made it."

"What's that?"

"We left some husky members of the Royal Canadian Mounted Police back there on the highway. The Mounties always get their man, don't they? Or men."

I said, "If you want them, why didn't you ask them for help when they stopped you?"

"I don't want them. You know perfectly well I can't

afford to get mixed up with the police."

I glanced at her. "Not even to save your child's life, ma'am?"

She flushed, and defended herself quickly: "They'd be more concerned with catching their criminals. Penny would be just an afterthought to them. You're the one who's supposed to be hired to protect her. That's why I came to you."

I said, "I wish you'd make up your mind. Last I heard, you weren't falling for my private-eye act at all. Now you've got me all confused."

"That," she said grimly, "makes two of us."

"And if you don't want the police, why drag them into the conversation?"

She was watching me thoughtfully. "I was just wondering why *you* don't want them, Mr. Clevenger. Under the circumstances, wouldn't a respectable private detective charged with responsibility for a young girl's life insist on notifying the authorities?"

It was a good question, but she'd left me an out and I took it: "The adjective is yours, ma'am. I can't recall ever having claimed to be respectable, if that means liking cops. I've been a private investigator too long to want to get mixed up with them. Back home I've got to cooperate with them if I'm to stay in business. I've got to take their lip and keep smiling politely. That's back home. Up here, to hell with them. I've lost no damn Canadian policemen and I'm not about to find any I don't have to. Okay?"

She was still studying my face. "You've got an answer

to everything, haven't you? So you're going to tackle two desperate, armed hoodlums singlehanded, with nothing but a little pine stick. You're either a brave man or a damn phony, Mr. Clevenger. I wish I knew which."

I said, "There's an easy way to find out."

She regarded me a moment longer, shrugged minutely, and turned away toward the truck and trailer waiting nearby on the little dirt track through the woods. I noted that she had an easy, almost sexless way of walking: the way of a self-confident woman who felt no need to do tricks with her hips to call attention to her femininity.

I called after her: "Mrs. Drilling."

She stopped and glanced back. "Yes?"

"What was your maiden name?" I already knew, of course, but for some reason I wanted to make it official.

"O'Brien," she said after a momentary pause. "Why?"

"Nothing," I said. "I was just curious. Lead on, Jenny O'Brien."

She started to speak, maybe to protest the familiarity, but then she laughed instead, and climbed into the pickup. I tested my sticky club once more, glanced at the Volkswagen more or less hidden among the trees, and went over and climbed into the trailer and closed the door. I heard the big truck engine start, up forward, and we were off.

It was a rough ride in the swaying, bouncing house trailer. Some plastic dishes almost clobbered me, spilling out of a high cabinet above me; and I could hear various foods and spices rubbing elbows behind the little doors that remained closed. It occurred to me to wonder if there might not be a nasty chemical reagent in there, somewhere, perhaps disguised as cooking oil or pancake syrup. The empty acid bottle I'd seen in Elaine's room wasn't proof that the entire supply had been used up. If there had been some left over, after Greg's treatment it could have been poured off and stored in a different container.

It didn't take me long to find it since the container had to be a rather special one—the stuff would go right through metal or plastic. A nice little salad-dressing jug with a glass stopper caught my eye almost at once. A drop of the contents on my finger sent me hurrying to the sink to wash it off; it wasn't olive oil.

I looked at the deceptive little bottle grimly. I guess I was kind of disillusioned. Somehow I'd got to thinking that Genevieve Drilling might possibly be just a nice, misunderstood lady after all. I considered pouring the stuff out and replacing it with water, just in case it might be used against me some time, but that's the kind of tricky protective maneuver that's apt to backfire, warning the subject that you're hep at just the moment when you're finally getting somewhere.

I also considered just diluting the reagent so it wouldn't be quite so powerful, but my chemistry is sketchy. I did remember that if you went about mixing it with water the wrong way it would spatter all over you, but I couldn't remember which was the right way, so finally I just stuck the bottle back among the groceries where I'd found it, the way I'd found it. I had just got the cupboard doors closed when our motion stopped.

Cautiously, I peeked out the side window, between the slats of the Venetian blind, and saw a blue lake lined with pines and firs. We seemed to be parked in a meadow that ran down to the shore. My pretty, freckled, truck-driving, acid lady had cut the switch, and the engine was silent. In accordance with my instructions, she didn't come back to keep me company, which was just as well. I might not have been able to resist the temptation to ask her to make me up a salad with her special dressing.

We just waited for visitors in our separate compartments, out there by the lake in the still Canadian forest, and after a while they came.

"In the truck, there! Hey, lady, wake up!" It was half a shout, half a hoarse, secretive whisper, from the edge of the nearby woods. I didn't risk showing myself at the window again. I just crouched near the trailer door, waiting. "All right, lady, now open both cab doors and get out so we can see what you've got in there… That's right. Just stand right there. One false move and the girl gets this knife right in the kidney. Okay, Mousie, go check the trailer."

I heard Genevieve's voice, with a nice edge of panic. "There isn't anybody in the trailer."

"There'd better not be. Go on, Mousie."

"Wait!" She sounded terrified. She was doing swell. I reminded myself that, where deceit was concerned, she'd had a professional instructor named Ruyter, and some practice along the way. "Wait!" she cried. "There is somebody! It's that private detective. I had to bring him! I couldn't help it. He stopped me and demanded to know where… where Penny was. I had to tell him. He was going to the police if I didn't tell him. He promised he wouldn't do anything to harm you as long as she was all right."

"He promised!" sneered the voice from the woods. "Now isn't that sweet!"

"You don't understand! He's just a private investigator, he doesn't care about you. He says the Canadian authorities can look after their own damn fugitives; he isn't being paid to do anything but look after Penny. Let him come out; let him talk to you. Don't hurt her just because… I couldn't help it, I tell you. I *had* to bring him. It was either him or the police."

There was a lengthy silence before the man out there spoke. "All right, tell him to come out with his hands in plain sight. If he flashes a gun, the kid is dead, understand?"

"Yes. Yes, of course. Come out Mr. Clevenger. Please be careful. He's got a knife in Penny's back."

I opened the door and stepped down to the ground. "Drop the stick!" said the youth holding Penny.

I could see him now, and his companion, and the girl. She was still wearing yesterday's short divided skirt and grubby white shirt. She was kind of mussed and dirty, with mud on her sneakers and bobbysox. Her hairnet was missing and the rollers and curlers were coming unwound, snakelike, here and there. Nevertheless, she didn't look to be fundamentally damaged, although her face was pale and scared behind the big glasses.

The men were in dungarees and work shirts. They were a mean-looking pair: one handsome, murderous young delinquent, and one aging sneak-thief with obvious alcoholic predilections.

"Drop the stick!" the younger one snarled.

"Go to hell, punk," I said pleasantly. "What are you afraid of, that I'll point it at you and say bang-bang-you're-dead?" I took a couple of steps away from the trailer door. "You with the bloodshot eyes," I said. "Come over here and take a look through this mobile home. Make sure I didn't bring any cops before your friend wets his pants worrying."

The younger one tightened his arm across Penny's throat. "Watch your lip, mister," he said. He hesitated, and said reluctantly, "All right, Mousie. Go ahead and look in there like I told you in the first place."

A signal passed between them that I guess I wasn't supposed to see or understand; then Mousie sidled past me. I heard him enter the trailer and come back out. "Okay, Frankie. It's empty."

"All right, you," said Frankie. "What did you have to say to us?"

"Let the kid go and we'll forget we ever saw you," I said, pretending not to hear the old thief slipping up behind me. The clumsy way he moved, it was no wonder he'd wound up in jail. I kept talking to help him out: "What do you say, Frankie? Turn her loose and we won't bother you. You can go where you damn well please."

Frankie said, "Bother? Tall man, you don't bother me a bit." Apparently American gangster movies had formed a large part of his education: or maybe all prisons turn out the same product the world over—well, the English-speaking world over. He had that tough, lipless, convict way of talking. "You mean we should let you drive off and leave us here on foot? That would be a hell of a deal, now. We might as well have stayed in Brandon."

I said, "All right, take the damn truck. Take the trailer. Just turn the kid loose. I promise…"

I pivoted on the word, and my timing was right. Mousie was right there, with the big kitchen knife raised as if to chip ice for a highball. I suppose he was really hoping to plant it between my shoulder blades. He might be a professional thief, but as a murderer he was strictly amateur talent. The high-held knife was out of position for any kind of thrust or parry. I was perfectly safe as I lunged with the stick and drove it into him just below the ribs. He doubled up, offering me the back of his head, and I whipped my little pine tree across the base of his skull, not too hard, and he fell down unconscious.

I swung back and said casually, "Like I was saying, Frankie, turn her loose. Before I come over there and spank you."

It had been a gamble, of course. I might not have tried it if Frankie had been holding a gun. Startled, he might have fired by mistake. But it's hard to do serious damage with a knife by mistake. The kid was still standing, biting her lip against the pain of the nervous knifepoint in her back.

"You shouldn't have done that, mister!" Frankie's face was shiny. "Drop the stick! I won't tell you again. Drop it or I'll—"

"You'll do what?" I said. "Kill her? What'll that get you?" I spat on the ground between us. "I'll tell you what it'll get you, punk. It'll get you dead. I've got longer legs than you and I know the woods real good. You so much as break the skin with that knife you're holding and I'll run you down and kill you. Now make up your mind. Turn her loose and I won't hurt you. Make me wait any longer and I'll take you apart and throw the pieces in the lake. Come on, Junior, don't just stand there trying to look tough. You may be tough for here, but down around Denver where I come from, little boys like you don't go out without their mothers." I looked at him for a moment longer, and made a sound of disgust. I threw the stick away from me. "There. No stick. *Now* what are you going to do, Sonnyboy?"

It worked. Not only had I knocked his partner unconscious, I'd also hurt his pride. I'd belittled him in front of two females. Furthermore, even his limited brain was capable of understanding, at last, that nothing he did to Penny was going to help him get the truck he badly needed to get away. It was me he had to kill, and he stepped around her to do it.

He came in with the knife. Unlike Mousie, he knew enough to hold it like a sword, not an icepick, but that was about all he knew. He came in cautiously at first, but when I gave ground he gained courage and tried a rush. I did it strictly by the book, moving quickly to his right and using a circular karate kick to disarm him. It's better to use the feet when dealing with a knife, since feet generally have shoes on them—in this case a fairly heavy boot, since I was dressed for camping.

The knife flew out of his grasp. The force of the kick spun him away from me, grasping his bruised hand. I kicked again, since I was in the footwork groove, and cut his legs out from under him. Then I stepped up and kicked him carefully in the head. I went over and got his knife and threw it into the lake. It wasn't worth saving: one of those crude imitation Bowies sold to the kind of hunters who think they need a big knife for protection from deer and rabbits.

I picked up the instrument Mousie had dropped and went over to where Genevieve stood with her arms about her daughter.

"I guess this belongs to you, ma'am," I said, holding out the long-bladed kitchen knife.

She patted the little girl on the shoulder and came forward to face me. There was a funny little pause. I put out of my mind all thought of the jug of acid I'd discovered in the trailer. Like Greg's death, or Elaine's, it had no real bearing on my mission here, which was to gain this woman's respect and friendship, and help her get wherever she wanted to go.

I had time to think that it couldn't have worked out better. Running into a pair of escaped prisoners had been a wild coincidence, but it had given me a chance to do my stuff—and whether Genevieve Drilling thought me a private dick or a secret agent, she couldn't help but feel a certain sense of obligation, I reflected, that might form the basis of a very satisfactory relationship.

She said, "You're quite a hero, Mr. Clevenger. That was quite a performance." Her voice had an odd, strained sound, as if she was balanced between tears and hysterical laughter. I was completely unprepared when she swung her arm and slapped me hard across the face. "You damn phony!" she cried.

12

Like the Marines and Boy Scouts, we're always supposed
to be prepared for anything, but I'll admit I was startled
enough that I stepped back with my hand to my face.
Maybe I even looked hurt, like a boy who'd thought
himself entitled to a goodnight kiss and found that his
young lady had contrary notions.

"Just what," I asked, "was that for?"

Genevieve laughed sharply. "Come now, Mr.
Clevenger, let's not carry the farce any farther. Do you
really think I'm stupid enough to believe in that little
ballet you just put on for my benefit?"

"But—"

"You're not really much of an actor, you know. It was so
obviously rehearsed! You should have made it look harder."

I said, "Look, ma'am—"

"You can skip the country accent, too," she snapped.
She looked at the two figures sprawled on the grass.
"Your friends must be very uncomfortable, lying there.

Why don't you tell them to get up and take their bows? They were quite good; they really had me believing they were escaped convicts, for a while. Until the sham battle started. That was most unconvincing, Mr. Clevenger. Do you know what it reminded me of? A story I read as a girl, by Sabatini or somebody. The crude villain wanted to gain the confidence of the highborn heroine, so he got a couple of his henchmen to fake an attack on her, after which he whipped out his trusty rapier and came charging to the rescue. The girl, being an ingenue type, fell into his arms oozing gratitude and admiration. Well, I'm not an ingenue type! I know a staged fight when I see one. You shouldn't have been so serenely confident beforehand, for one thing. You and that silly pine stick! And the way you turned at just the right moment, when that man was going to stab you from behind. I was about to scream a warning, but I suppose he gave you a signal of some kind."

"No," I said, "but Penny did. When her eyes got wide enough, I knew it was time to turn."

She laughed, quite unconvinced. "You always have an answer, don't you. Well, don't waste your ingenuity on me any longer. It was a cruel and vicious deception, Mr. Clevenger. I suppose sooner or later we'll hear of the *real* convicts being captured in Labrador or British Columbia. Come on, darling, let's go."

She started to take Penny's arm. Then, as an afterthought she swung back, snatched the kitchen knife from her hand, tossed it into the trailer, and slammed the door shut. I suppose I could have made sounds of protest, but I could see it would be a waste of time. She'd convinced herself it was all a fraud. Perhaps she'd wanted to convince herself, since it relieved her of the burden of gratitude. Some people can always find good reasons for not honoring their debts, I reflected sourly, as I watched mother and daughter march to the truck and drive away.

I had to admit, however, that I was hardly in a position to scrutinize other people's motives too closely. I'd saved the kid from a pair of perfectly genuine thugs, but my reasons could hardly be called straightforward and honest. The thought didn't comfort me greatly. It was a long hike through the woods back to the Volkswagen. When I got there, Johnston was sitting on the fender smoking a big cigar.

"The Drillings drove by half an hour ago, looking smug and self-righteous," he said as I limped up. "Larry's on their tail, if he hasn't got lost. I suppose somebody's got to break in the awkward ones, but why does it always have to be me? If I get this one back in one piece, it will be a miracle." He frowned as if he'd said too much, and went on quickly: "I figured I'd better be the one to talk to you, since you and my partner don't seem to take to each other. Don't want you hauling out that little knife again. Well, what happened to you? What's been going on back in there?"

"Go to hell," I said.

He took the cigar from his mouth and looked at me bleakly. "Look, Clevenger, I've got one man on this

job I have to baby, but I sure as hell don't have to baby
you. Don't give me any trouble or I'll lower the boom,
and don't think I can't. Now tell me what this monkey
business is all about."

I told him, and after I'd convinced him I hadn't made
it up, he thought it was very funny. Well, I guess it was.
After a day or two I found myself able to laugh at it, too,
but that still didn't get me the trusting relationship with
Genevieve Drilling and her friend Ruyter that I was under
strict orders to establish.

Not that Ruyter gave any further indication of his
presence as we made our way east to Lake Superior and
then drove about the Great Lakes by the northern route
that runs far up into the big woods. Hans was probably
piloting his fancy Mercedes fast along the shorter lake-
shore route, I reflected as I followed the shiny silver trailer
endlessly along the tree-lined highway. He'd want to get
east before Drilling to make any getaway preparations
that might be necessary. I hoped he'd do a good job so I
wouldn't have to.

It was a long, dull drive. There's a lot of country up
there, but you can't see it for the trees. The highway
hardly ever climbed out of the dense green stuff to give
you a real view of it. There wasn't even a moose to
break the monotony of the interminable evergreen forest,
although there were plenty of signs telling us to watch out
for the big beasts—like deer-crossing signs back home.

Averaging some three hundred miles a day, camping
at night, we crossed the province of Ontario and entered

the province of Quebec. Here we hit French signs and road markers, and gas station attendants who could barely communicate in English. I'd been out of the United States for the better part of a week by this time, but only now did I begin to feel that I'd entered a foreign country.

There was even that hint of tension you often find abroad these days. There were occasional phrases chalked or painted on shacks and barns along the highway indicating that somebody thought it would be nice if the English-speaking usurpers went away and left the French-speaking true owners of the soil in peace. It wasn't my fight, but I couldn't help thinking this might seem kind of funny to a red-skinned gent brought up speaking, say, one of the Algonquian tongues that had once been current in the neighborhood. Contrary to popular opinion, Indians have a real sharp sense of humor.

It was raining again as we approached Montreal: we'd been playing tag with the same storm clear across the country. Having been brought up in the arid southwest, I tire of precipitation very quickly. This is particularly true when I have to spend more than a night or two in soggy blankets in a leaky tent. I guess I've spent enough time being uncomfortable outdoors that I no longer feel I'm accomplishing anything praiseworthy by proving I can take it.

Apparently Mrs. Drilling and daughter, although better equipped, felt much the same way, because they stopped at a trailer park on the outskirts of the city, made arrangements to desert their rolling home for the night, and drove in to register at the fanciest hotel in town. At least that was one possible explanation for their action. I didn't dismiss the possibility, however, that Mrs. Drilling might have other reasons for staying at the Queen Mary than just the desire to soak in a real tub and eat a meal she hadn't cooked herself.

Whatever her motives, I was glad for the chance to clean up in civilized surroundings, after spending too many mornings shaving out of a saucepan with mosquitoes chewing at my neck and ears. By paying for more accommodations than I really needed—well, Uncle Sam would get the bill eventually—I managed to get a room right down the hall from the Drilling menage. It would have been pleasant to have a leisurely drink and then spend plenty of time in the tiled bath, as Mrs. Drilling was probably doing, but I reminded myself that duty came before luxury, and made myself respectable as fast as possible. I guess I had a hunch that there might be some action, now that we'd put the great northern wilderness behind us.

It came almost before I'd finished buttoning my only white shirt and tying a conservative knot in my only necktie—I hadn't figured on needing much formal attire on the Black Hills job. The knock on the door had a timid sound, but I took the usual precautions answering it, remembering that both Elaine and Greg had been careless with doors.

But the kid in the doorway had nothing in her hands. She looked up at me through her hornrimmed glasses, and showed me a mouthful of stainless steel in what was obviously meant to be a pretty smile.

"I hope you don't mind… I mean, may I come in?" she said.

The first thing I noticed, after stepping back to let her enter, was that she'd finally got everything off her head except the hair. It was the first time since we'd met that I'd seen her without either curlers or some sort of patent covering of net or plastic or both. Unveiled and liberated, the hair hardly seemed worthy of all this protective concern. It didn't glow like neon, or spell out messages in Urdu, or dance the Twist around her scalp.

It was just normal, healthy, light-brown, young-girl hair, done up in a big puffball arrangement that made her face look very small, with tiny childish features. She was really a pretty kid, I realized, despite the glasses and braces—and kid wasn't quite the word, either.

I mean, she was wearing honest-to-God nylons and grownup white pumps with moderately high heels and little white gloves. Her dress was that kind of beltless, shapeless model that was known as a sack a few years ago and is now back in favor, I understand, under the title of shift. Whatever the name, it's a style that mostly looks like hell on older women, but being nice and simple, it can often look very cute on the young ones.

This was a jumper job, blue, with a ruffly, semi-transparent white blouse taking over the coverage duty at neck and arms. The straight dress made contact with her body only infrequently, but often enough to make it plain that while she might still technically be considered a child, the condition wasn't going to last very much longer. I'd closed the door with the two of us inside. Now, after looking her over, I gave an admiring whistle. I guess I was teasing her, but after all, it was a real improvement over the grubby jeans, shorts, and bastard pant-skirt outfits in which she'd been traveling. It deserved a little applause.

She turned pink and looked uncomfortable, and glanced nervously around the room, saw the two big beds, and looked away. She'd heard about beds. I gathered that, visiting a strange man's hotel room alone, she wasn't at all certain she wasn't going to get raped—and I had a hunch, despite her wary attitude, that she wasn't entirely certain it wouldn't be an interesting and worthwhile experience. She was young enough to be scared, but she was also old enough to be curious.

I said, "I gather you haven't come to see me because you want me to take you back to your dad. That's hardly a long-distance traveling costume you've got on."

"No-no. I…" There was a little pause while she looked down at her pretty white pumps, with her pretty white gloves—or the small hands therein—gripping each other nervously. "I don't believe it!" she said abruptly, looking at me. "I told Mummy from the start I didn't believe it and I still don't!"

"What don't you believe?"

"That fight," she said. "I don't believe you faked it. And those men. I'm sure they were real convicts. I was with them longer than Mummy, going through the woods; I heard them talking. They weren't putting on an act for me, I know they weren't!"

I said, "Honey, you don't have to convince me. Have you told your mother this?"

"Of course I have!" Penny flushed. "Mummy says I'm just being silly. She says I'm just a big gullible baby. She says you're a very clever government agent, not a private detective at all, and that you're not to be trusted for one little minute."

I laughed. "That sounds like your ma, all right. And what do you think, Penny?"

She studied her toes again. "I… I think that if there's even a chance that you did save us from those men, all alone with nothing but a little stick, then you're a… pretty brave person, aren't you, Mr. Clevenger? And we owe you a great deal, don't we? And we should at least give you a chance to prove your good faith, shouldn't we? That's the least we can do. Maybe I *am* just being silly and naïve. Maybe you are just a cold, calculating…!" She stopped, embarrassed.

"A cold, calculating what?" I asked, grinning. "Sneak, snooper, fink? What was your mother's descriptive term for me?"

Penny looked shocked. "Oh, Mummy'd never say fink! She won't let me say it even though all the other kids back home…" She stopped, realizing that she was drifting from the subject. She looked up at me with sudden, disconcerting steadiness. "Mummy says you don't *really* care what happens to me, and neither does Daddy. She says it's just an excuse so you can keep an eye on us for your government agency, whatever it is."

It was my turn to be embarrassed, watched by the steady blue eyes behind the hornrimmed glasses. I wished again, as I had before, that Mrs. Drilling had had the good sense to leave her offspring out of this. It was not a business for little girls, even little girls in grownup nylons and high heels. I made a show of shrugging my shoulders helplessly.

"It's impossible to convince someone who doesn't want to be convinced, Penny," I said, sounding pompous and fatherly.

"And it's very easy to convince somebody who does want to be convinced, isn't it? Particularly if they're... well, kind of young."

She was still watching me closely. She was a bright little girl. She was also, I thought, a lonely little girl, needing reassurance badly.

I said, "If you want to call your father long distance, there's the phone. Of course, if I'm lying, then he'll have been briefed to lie, too, won't he?"

She made a face. "That's not much help."

I said, "Hell, honey, there's never any help of the kind you're looking for. It's up to you. Either I'm a liar and a phony or I'm not. Don't ask me to make up your damn little mind for you."

After a moment she grinned. "It's hardly a question of my damn little mind, Mr. Clevenger. It's a question

of my mother's damn little mind, isn't it? She's the one
you want to convince." Penny drew a long breath. "Well,
come to dinner with us and convince her."

I guess I looked surprised, which was all right. I was
supposed to look surprised. I said, "What?"

"That's what I came to tell you. Maybe you're a phony
and maybe you aren't, but if you did help us, back there in
the woods, then you deserve a hearing. Well, you've got
one. I pestered Mummy until she agreed to sit down and
talk it over with you in a civilized way. We're all having
dinner downstairs in the Voyageur Club at seven-thirty."
She glanced at the little gold watch on her wrist. "That
gives you just about half an hour to dig up some good
evidence, Mr. Clevenger. Don't be late."

13

The Voyageur Club is to Montreal, I guess, what Stallmästaregården is to Stockholm or Antoine's is to New Orleans—to drop the names of a couple of classy restaurants I've been forced to visit in the line of duty. I found it a large, rambling, dimly-lighted room on the ground floor of the hotel. The waiters were dressed like oldtime French-Canadians about to embark on a fur-trading expedition into the primitive American wilderness. There were old utensils and weapons hanging on the walls.

It was the kind of atmosphere that could seem either contrived and fakey, or just pleasantly and comfortably old-fashioned, depending on the skill with which it was handled and whether or not it was used to cover up deficiencies in the culinary department. My first impression was favorable, but I reserved judgment until I could see the service and taste the food.

Mrs. Drilling and Miss Drilling were already

established at a table when I entered from the lobby. Before my eyes became accustomed to the darkness, I had a little trouble telling them apart from across the room. They were dressed identically: Genevieve was wearing a jumper and blouse just like Penny's, and her hair was also combed up big. In theory, I suppose these mother-and-daughter outfits are a cute idea. In practice they never seem to work out well except on magazine covers; I suppose because a thirty-five-year-old woman isn't likely to look her best in something that makes a fifteen-year-old kid look like a living doll.

Genevieve looked up when I stopped by the table. Her eyes didn't exactly display the warm light of eager hospitality. She waited for me to speak.

I said, "This is real kind of you, ma'am."

She said in a neutral voice, "It wasn't my idea. My gullible daughter seems to be suffering from an acute attack of hero-worship. She's at the impressionable age."

"Oh, Mummy!" said Penny, pained.

"Sit down, Mr. Clevenger," Genevieve said. "The counsel for the defense has made me promise you a fair hearing, but maybe we should have a drink before you present your evidence and your arguments to the court."

"Yes, ma'am," I said, seating myself between the two ladies. "Reckon I could go for a martini, ma'am."

"Oh, no!" Genevieve protested. "Not a martini, Mr. Clevenger! That doesn't go with your Western act at all. Bourbon and branch water should be your tipple, or corn whiskey straight from the jug."

"Oh, Denver is a real modern city these days," I said. "We've got martinis and juvenile delinquents just like the rest of the country. And you don't sound as if you were approaching my case with an open mind, Judge Drilling, ma'am."

Penny said, "That's right, Mummy. You could at least *try* to sound unprejudiced."

Genevieve laughed. She was quite a pretty woman, I realized again, and her little-girl jumper costume didn't really go so badly with her wholesome, freckled type of good looks.

"All right," she said. "I'll try. Order me a martini, too, please, Mr. Clevenger, and a coke for Penny. Is it still raining out? I must say, it would be nice to see a little sunshine for a change…"

We talked about the weather, and the country, and the roads we'd covered, and the fierce competitive spirit that seemed to burn, torch-like, in all Canadian drivers.

"It wouldn't be so bad if they'd just get out ahead and *stay* there!" Genevieve complained. "The minute you pass one, he's got to get back around you—but then he goes right to sleep again! So you've got to pass him again or poke along behind him at forty. By the time I've maneuvered sixteen feet of trailer around the same motorized cluck for the third time in ten miles, I'm ready to run him right off the road."

"Well, you handle that rig like an expert, ma'am," I said.

"I ought to," she said. "My father was a contractor.

There wasn't a piece of machinery he used that I wasn't checked out on, Mr. Clevenger—that is, until we got rich and respectable and I was supposed to stay off the trucks and cats and look ladylike in a pale blue convertible with an automatic shift—" She broke off, and gave me a sharp glance. "You're a real confidence man, aren't you? You know just how to flatter a woman and get her talking about herself."

"Sure," I said. "Nothing softens them up like telling them they're swell truck-drivers. I've found the technique infallible, ma'am."

She laughed reluctantly, and stopped laughing. "Well, let's have it," she said. "I suppose you have a lot of phony identification cards and things that are supposed to convince me you aren't working for Uncle Sam in some clever and underhanded way."

Penny said, "Oh, Mummy! You promised you'd—"

"It's all right, darling," Genevieve said. "Mr. Clevenger has a tough hide, I'm sure. He doesn't mind my needling him a little. Well, Mr. Clevenger? Should we start with your private detective's license or permit or whatever you call it?" I showed it to her. She glanced at it and said, "A very handsome piece of work. Now, how about a pistol permit? You do have one, don't you, even though you don't have the gun with you? And a few credit cards, perhaps. Although that's pretty weak. Even I could get myself a credit card in the name of Clevenger if I wanted to."

Penny stirred uncomfortably. "Mummy, you're not being *fair*."

"Oh, I'm being very fair," her mother said. "Mr. Clevenger knows perfectly well that his documents mean nothing because any government agent could have them made up for any character he cared to impersonate. He's going to have to come up with better evidence than this." She smiled and patted her daughter's hand. "The fact that his Douglas Fairbanks routine is irresistible to teen-age girls hardly constitutes proof of his good intentions, darling."

I said, "Well, what about this, Mrs. Drilling?"

She looked at the paper I held out—a folded newspaper clipping—and at me. Then she took the clipping and unfolded it, frowned, studied it carefully, and looked up again suspiciously.

"I didn't see this item anywhere," she said. "I'd certainly have noticed it."

"Maybe you weren't looking at the right Winnipeg paper shortly after that little ruckus in the woods, ma'am. I just happened to come across it. Somebody'd left it behind at a roadside cafe."

This wasn't true, of course. Figuring I might have a chance to use it sooner or later, I'd phoned Mac to put somebody at tracking down all published news items bearing on the subject. They'd been rushed to a pickup spot—drop, if you want to be technical—here in Montreal as soon as it became clear we'd be passing through the city.

Penny was frowning at us. "What is it?"

"Oh, a little item I just knocked out on my portable

printing press," I said. "It purports to be a news picture of two convicts who were recaptured in a rather battered state a few days after their escape from the penitentiary at Brandon. Strictly counterfeit, of course, like all my documents. As your mother said back there, sooner or later we'll hear of the *real* escapees being taken in Labrador or British Columbia."

"Let me see!" The girl took the clipping from her mother's hand. "But those *are* the two men who tried to—"

I said, "Honey, don't look now but you're being naïve. Naturally, if I'm going to fake a picture, I'll use faces you'll recognize. Look at your ma. She doesn't believe a word of it. And don't think she'll go hunting through old newspaper files to check it, either. She knows what she knows, and nothing's going to convince her otherwise." I sighed. "It's no use, Penny. I thank you for your good offices, but the court has already passed judgment and isn't about to reverse its verdict."

Penny turned indignantly to Genevieve. "But *Mummy*—"

"Let me see that again," Genevieve said. She frowned at the clipping for several seconds. Then she looked at me. "If that picture *is* genuine, I owe you an apology, don't I, Mr. Clevenger?"

"If," I said.

"Well," she said, "is it?"

"Yes, ma'am," I said. "It is."

She hesitated. "I don't trust you," she said at last. "I don't trust you one little bit." Then she drew a long breath. "But I'll admit it begins to look as if I'd been a little hasty. What Penny had to say about those men, and now this clipping… maybe you really did help us out of a very nasty situation, Mr. Clevenger. If so, please forgive me for jumping to conclusions."

It was a pretty good apology, as apologies go. I mean, she'd hedged a little, but on the whole I should have been pleased and satisfied—and I would have been, if I hadn't found myself wondering just how long she'd been sitting on that speech before she'd found an excuse to deliver it. I had a sudden strong feeling that the whole scene had been planned in advance: that I'd been brought here by the daughter so the mother could apologize to me on one pretext or another, if not a newspaper clipping then something else.

It was a snide thought, but I found confirmation when I glanced at Penny's face. Instead of jumping up and down happily because her hero had been vindicated, she was looking uncomfortable and embarrassed, as if she wished herself miles away where she wouldn't have to watch her mother putting on a humble act for a man for some obscure adult reason.

I didn't spend too much time worrying about the reason. It promised to be an interesting evening, and it was starting out well. Once we got over the little awkwardness that followed Genevieve's apology, everything went gracefully. The service was smooth and efficient and the drinks were excellent. The salmon was as good as a fish can be, and you forget how good that is when you live away from the ocean for a while.

Penny was allowed a glass of wine with her meal, and presently, not much to my surprise, she showed signs of getting sleepy and was given the room key and sent up to bed. I ordered a cognac and Genevieve took something green and sweet and minty. She raised her glass to me.

"Well, Mr. Clevenger?" she murmured.

"Well what, Mrs. Drilling?" I said.

She was smiling wryly. "Were we too obvious? We haven't had much practice at intrigue, you know. I think Penny did rather well, don't you?"

I studied her face for a moment. I said, "With a little practice, she'll be another Mata Hari—but don't forget that lady got shot. Two people have already died on this operation. Why not let me take the kid back to papa before she gets hurt playing in a grownup game?"

Genevieve grimaced. "You're a stubborn man, Clevenger. You're still pretending to be a silly private eye. Please stop it."

I said, "I thought we decided—"

"We decided that those men back there may have been real convicts, and you may have saved us from them very bravely and skillfully. That satisfied Penny, but you and I both know that it has nothing to do with what kind of an agency you're working for, public or private. In fact, if it *was* a real fight, and you're so good you can take on two desperate criminals practically barehanded and dispose of them without even breathing hard, then you're too good to be working for some cheap little Denver detective bureau, Mr. Clevenger or whatever your name is. No matter how you slice it, it comes up stamped U.S."

"Your flattering estimate of government men might surprise a few people," I said. "And in that case, why the humble apology and the free meal?"

"Because I still need help," she said. "Or maybe I should say that I need help again, very badly, and again you're the only man I can turn to. I don't care who you're working for. If you're a government man, you may even be able to talk me into giving your lousy scientific papers back, but first you have to do something for me."

It was a real swifty. The last thing I wanted was to be handed Dr. Drilling's papers: they had to be delivered by her and Ruyter.

I said, "Take the proposition to Johnston and his sidekick, ma'am. They'll snap at it. Me, I'm not being paid to hunt secret documents, any more than escaped convicts. My experience is that any private character who gets mixed up with stuff like that, winds up in trouble, even if he's trying to be helpful. Johnston and Fenton are the names. You've undoubtedly seen them along the road. If you want, I'll bring them around for a conference."

She shook her head impatiently. "Oh, why don't you stop that stupid pretense... I couldn't talk to those two clowns and you know it."

I said, "Johnston's no clown. I won't say as much for his partner, but Johnston's a smart operative, don't kid yourself."

"Just the same, he wouldn't deal. I know the type. He'd make no concessions. He'd just start waving the flag and telling me about my patriotic duty, in between threats."

I gave her a quick glance. "And you think I'm a government man but you think I won't? You think I'll deal? How will I deal?"

She hesitated and looked down at her green drink. "I think you're a smart man, Mr. Clevenger."

"Sure," I said. "Thanks. What does that mean?"

She said slowly, "I told you my father was a fairly successful contractor. I think you're a smart man, and I know I'm a fairly rich woman, and... and not too unattractive, I hope."

There was a little silence. I said, "Let's not be so damn subtle, Jenny O'Brien. Are you trying to bribe me, or seduce me, or both?"

She looked up and smiled. "Well, what's your weakness, Dave, money or sex?"

I drew a long breath and said, "I always thought money was a highly overrated commodity, ma'am."

14

Leaving the elevator, we walked down the hall, passing the door to Jenny's room. I had to start thinking of her as Jenny now. It wasn't possible to consider playing a seduction scene with a woman with the cold and formal name of Genevieve.

She didn't say anything about checking to see if her daughter had made it safely. I guess she felt it was no time to act motherly; besides, a fifteen-year-old girl wasn't likely to get lost between lobby and hotel room. We stopped at my door. Jenny put a hand on my arm.

"Dave." Her voice sounded hesitant.

"What?"

"You're going to have… to give me the cues. I haven't had much experience at this sort of thing."

I glanced at her sharply, a little disappointed in her. I don't mean that I'd been taking her proposition at face value: I hadn't. It was fairly obvious that she had something tricky in mind, whether or not it actually involved a bed. I couldn't legitimately complain about that. We were all being pretty tricky on this job. I just didn't like being treated as if I were a moron who'd swallow anything. That innocent-little-me line, from a woman her age with her record, was getting us pretty far out into the cornfield, I felt.

Surprisingly, I saw that for all of being a married woman with a teenage daughter—not to mention all the other things she probably was—she did look kind of innocent. I don't mean the fragile, helpless, frightened kind of innocence. She looked like a healthy, freckled, tomboy who'd finally been run down and put into shoes and a pretty dress, and who thought it was kind of crazy, but was perfectly willing to give womanhood a whirl if somebody'd just show her how. It bothered me. She kept stepping out of character—the character my evidence said she ought to have, the character the acid bottle in her trailer said she ought to have.

"I mean," she went on, "I've never seduced anybody before. You'll have to show me how it goes."

Well, it was a moderately fresh angle from which to attack an ancient situation. I guess it beat the sultry-siren routine at that. I unlocked the door, opened it, and reached inside to switch on the room light before speaking.

Then I said, "I seem to recall hearing your name linked with that of a man once. A man named Ruyter. Probably a vicious slander."

She glanced at my sarcasm, hesitated, but walked on past me without making a response. I followed her inside and closed the door. She turned to face me in the center of the room.

"I didn't say I was a virgin, Dave."

"So?"

"So I'm married, I've had a child, and maybe I've even slept with a man who wasn't my husband. A man who was charming and attentive and very, very persistent. Maybe I was even silly enough to believe, at first, that his persistence was due to my irresistible beauty and fascinating personality." Her tone was wry. After a moment she went on: "Arid maybe one night when my husband was supposed to take me out and I'd got all dressed up only to get the usual last-minute call from the lab—Howard didn't even bother to call himself, he had his assistant do it—maybe I just got good and mad and called up Hans and let him buy me an expensive dinner and lure me to his place afterwards." She was silent; then she looked up almost shyly and said, "That isn't quite the same, Dave, as coldbloodedly arranging to spend the night with a man I hardly know and don't trust at all."

"Thanks," I said.

"Well, I don't trust you and I'm not going to pretend I do. I'm quite sure, for instance, that you're here not only because a woman has made you a proposition you find moderately intriguing, but also because you feel it your duty to your government—all right, your employers, let's not argue about who they are—to learn what's behind her offer." She studied me shrewdly. I didn't say anything. She sighed and said, "Not that I ever had a great deal of faith in Hans, either, but don't tell him that. Of course I pretended to be madly in love with him. It made the whole thing seem more dignified and graceful, and you don't tell a reasonably nice man—well, I thought he was reasonably nice at the time; an obvious, international-type smoothie, but a nice smoothie—that you're just sleeping with him because he's available and you're mad at your husband."

I said, "For not having much faith in this international smoothie, you're sure going a long way with him now. Could this have something to do with what you need help with?"

"It could, but let's not talk about it yet," she said. "I mean, it isn't very romantic. Right now I'm supposed to be overwhelming you with my charm, not boring you with my troubles." She hesitated. "Dave."

"Yes."

"Be nice," she said softly. "Play up a little, please. You're making it very hard for me. Don't act so government-agentish. Can't you see I'm embarrassed as hell?" She drew a sharp little breath and went on briskly before I could speak: "All right, now I've got as far as the man's hotel room. What do I do next, seduction-wise? Do I simply take off my clothes and jump into bed and stretch out my naked arms to him? It seems a little… well, abrupt. Shouldn't we first maybe have a couple of drinks?"

I said, "Shouldn't we first maybe discuss just what kind of help you're hoping to buy with your white body?"

She drew another quick breath and said impatiently:

"You're really being damned difficult! Even though I don't trust your motives at all, I'm willing to gamble on your being honest enough to do something for me after… after you've had me. Why can't you be willing to gamble on my being sensible enough not to ask more of you than… than one good lay is worth? Believe me, after living for fifteen odd years with a man who considers sex infinitely less interesting than science, I'm not likely to overvalue what I've got to offer."

I regarded her with growing respect, and the uneasy feeling that somewhere beneath the play-acting was some kind of a solid foundation of truth and sincerity. The question was, what kind.

"I said, "You do put it right on the line, Irish."

She met my look steadily. "I try to. I'm not going to ask you to betray your country or neglect your duty or anything like that. I… I just want somebody in my corner when the showdown comes, somebody who has a personal interest in seeing that I get a reasonably fair deal. I'm glad you didn't ask for money. I'd never be sure of a man to whom I'd given money."

I said, "You don't know much about this kind of business, do you? What makes you think a man who's willing to go for a deal on the side is going to stay bought no matter what you pay him off with?"

She shook her head quickly. "You don't understand. I'm not really asking you to be bought or stay bought, Dave Clevenger. All I'm really trying to do is get you to look at me as *me*, not as a bunch of damaging information in a file somewhere. If you'd just take one good look at me, forgetting everything you've heard, you'd see I couldn't possibly be the sinister person you think I am—you, and those two other government men who are following me so tenaciously, and Howard, and Hans, and… and everybody. I'm not that wicked and I'm not that clever."

She was really very good. I thought of a glove and a bottle that was supposed to contain salad dressing and didn't. I said, "I don't know what's more dangerous, a woman who tells you how wicked she is, or a woman who tells you how wicked she isn't."

Jenny made a protesting gesture. "Damn it, you're thinking of me as a movie cliché: espionage heavy, female, Type B. I'm not a cliché, I'm a woman, and a pretty ordinary woman at that. If I have to pay you or go to bed with you to make you realize that… Ah, let's get on with it! Where do you keep your liquor? That should be the first step, shouldn't it, to get the man drunk and susceptible?"

"Sure," I said. "That's the procedure. Here."

I went to my suitcase and got out a bottle of Scotch in a paper bag. As I slipped it out of the sack, I remembered the last time I'd had a drink from that bottle, and who'd been with me that night and what had happened between us, and what had happened to her later. It made me, for some reason, feel kind of cheap and disloyal.

I said to Jenny, "I didn't expect to be doing any entertaining up here, or I'd have had ice ready. Do you want me to ring for some?"

"No, let's not have bellboys crashing the party. I can drink it warm if you can." She took the glass I gave her and looked at me appraisingly. "Now you'd better sit down in that chair, so I can perch seductively on the arm, and then slither, down into your lap and snuggle up to you and get you all aroused."

I said, "The hell with that. You're too big a girl to sit on anybody's lap. If there's any lap-sitting to be done, let's wake up Penny. She's got the size for it if not the age and experience."

"Penny might surprise you," Jenny said. There was an odd note in her voice. I looked at her, and she laughed quickly and said, "Sometimes I just wonder how much my daughter knows about life first-hand. But I suppose all parents wonder that."

"She's kind of a sweet kid," I said.

Jenny drank from her glass and looked up irritably. "Damn it, we didn't come here to discuss my offspring! Come on, Dave, please give me some help. What do I do next to get this man into bed with me, and what happens about the clothes? I always wondered how in the world a woman got her girdle off with reasonable dignity at the critical moment."

"You shouldn't be wearing a girdle," I said. "Very poor technique. There are other ways of holding up your stockings. And who said anything about dignity?" I looked at her and frowned. "Hell, wasn't either Howard or Hans ever in in a hurry, Irish?"

She grimaced. "Oh, dear, no! They were both perfect

gentlemen at all times, damn them. Very considerate and patient… Look here, Dave Clevenger, is there something wrong with me? Here I am, offering to be as drunk and disorderly and sexy as you like, and all you do is ask stupid questions. Either you help me get this seduction off the ground and onto the mattress, or I'll go back to my room and get some sleep." She glared at me. "We've been in this room together for half an hour—well, it seems like half an hour—and you haven't even kissed me."

The moment of truth and sincerity had passed. We were back out where the tall corn grew—asking to be kissed, for God's sake.

I said, "Well, if you insist…" I stepped forward and kissed her on the mouth. The drinks we were both holding made it a rather awkward and cautious osculation. "Okay?" I said, stepping back.

She shrugged. "It depends on what you expect from a kiss. But now you've made a gesture in the right direction, Professor, proceed with the lesson."

I said, "There are two approaches you can use. There's the gradual-loss-of-inhibitions approach, and then there's the slaves-of-sudden-passion routine. The first takes more time and liquor, but the second's apt to be kind of hard on the costume. I mean, in one case you disrobe little by little, ostensibly for comfort's sake, as the orgy progresses, until you're down to fundamentals and things start happening. In the other case, after a short buildup, desire grips you all of a sudden and you drag the guy down on the nearest bed. Between the two of you, you manage to get off what's got to come off, and it may not all come off intact, if you know what I mean. If you've got a distance to go afterwards, and people to meet, and no safety pins handy, it can get awkward."

She was silent for a little. I wondered if she was telling herself to be a brave girl and go through with the horrid performance, now she'd carried it this far.

She said, "Well, I haven't got far to go, just down the hall, but these are the only reasonably good clothes I've got and… and Penny may be awake when I come in. Let's try the version that's easier on the wardrobe. What comes off first, the shoes or the dress?"

"Oh, the dress, by all means," I said. "Leave the shoes on as long as possible. Most men find the combination of high heels and lingerie very stimulating… Hold it!"

She'd gulped down the remains of her drink and set the glass aside. Now she was reaching around back for her zipper. She looked up, perplexed.

"What's the matter?"

"Where's your psychology? Let the man do the work, always. He probably wants to. Most men get a kick out of helping a woman take her clothes off. Turn around."

After a slight hesitation, she turned her back to me. I unhooked and unzipped the blue linen jumper and unbuttoned the thin white blouse underneath. The buttons were small and round and my fingers weren't quite steady, which annoyed me. It was strictly a mechanical reaction. I mean, I didn't really want the damn woman at all. I guess I had some sentimental notion of being true, at least a little longer, to a girl who was dead; besides, as far as I could see, it would be an additional and useless complication to an already complex situation. Genevieve Drilling wasn't a complete fool. Sleeping with me wouldn't change her opinion of me in any way that really mattered.

"There you are," I said, working the stuff off her shoulders. I couldn't help noticing that these were strong but nicely rounded, and freckled like her face. "It's legitimate to hang it up neatly at this stage of the proceedings," I said as, having stepped out of the dress and slipped her arms out of the blouse, she stood holding the garments a little uncertainly. "Later, of course, we'll be scattering things around in an uninhibited way... What's the matter?"

She'd swung back to face me. "You might at least take off your coat," she said with some resentment. "I feel awfully bare like this, with you standing there with coat and tie on. Here, I'll help you."

I watched her step up to me, in her high-heeled pumps and a white slip with a lot of finely pleated stuff at top and bottom, that rippled as she moved. They can do some very pretty things with pleats these days. She was a tall girl and she moved nicely. Well, I'd noticed that before.

I said, "Irish."

Her fingers were busy with the knot of my tie. She didn't look up. "Yes?"

"This is a lousy game, Irish. What are you hoping to win by it?"

The direct question startled her. Her fingers stopped

working, and she had to grab at the dress and blouse draped over her arm, to keep them from sliding off to the floor, but she still didn't look up. When she spoke, her voice was expressionless.

"I don't know what you mean."

"You're batting in the wrong league, doll," I said, making my voice hard. "I've had this one pulled on me before."

She said lightly, "Well, we're getting somewhere! At least you aren't calling me ma'am any more."

I said, "Okay, have it your way."

She yanked my tie free and looked up at last. "I told you—"

"I know. When the showdown comes, you want a friend in your corner at any cost. Okay, let's be friends. Here, take my coat, too. You can be hanging things up while I freshen the drinks." There was a little pause while she moved away and came back. Busy with the bottle, I glanced at her over my shoulder. "Now you can start moving in on one of the beds, Irish. Don't be obvious about it. Just act as if that happened to be the handiest place to sit."

"Like this?"

I went over and looked down at her sitting there. I didn't want to like her, and I didn't. It's hard to feel tenderness for a lady who keeps vitriol in the pantry. I didn't want to be attracted to her, either, but a goodlooking woman with her dress off is always attractive to a certain type of lewd male mind, and I'm afraid my mind happens to be just that type… I shoved one glass into her hand, and took a drink from the other one.

"Hell, you're much too ladylike, even in your underwear, Drilling," I said. "You're supposed to be getting tight, remember? Shove your legs out straight and let them wander well apart; let that slip ride up… That's better. Now muss your hair a little and drop a strap off your shoulder. Lick your lips. That's the girl. A little pouty now, kind of sleepily provocative…" I stepped back and surveyed the effect like a photographer posing a fashion model, with my head cocked to the side. "Very good, Irish. We'll make a tart of you yet."

She tossed the displaced lock of hair out of her eyes and looked up at me reproachfully. "You're making fun of me, aren't you?"

"Sure," I said. "Aren't you making fun of me, doll? Aren't you laughing silently at the stupid man who'd fall for a corny gag like this?" I made a face and mimicked: "Please show me how to seduce you, Mr. Clevenger, 'cause I'm just a little girl and don't know how."

She made no response to this. She just watched me sit down beside her. Then she asked quietly, "What have you had pulled on you before, Dave? What did you mean by that?"

"You know what I meant," I said. "If you want the details, there was a girl in… Well, never mind where." Actually, it had happened in Kiruna, Sweden, but Jenny'd want to know what a Denver private detective had been doing up there above the Arctic Circle and it was too late at night to figure out a plausible lie. I went on: "This girl had some friends. The friends wanted something from my hotel room. Her job was to keep me busy and interested while they got it. Like you're keeping me busy and interested now. What's happening in *your* hotel room, Irish?"

It was a long shot, but a faint narrowing of her eyes told me it had hit close. "Did she get it?" Jenny asked quickly. "I mean, did her friends get it?"

"Sure they got it," I said. "I wanted them to get it. It was a plant, but they didn't know that."

I used the word deliberately, to see what reaction I would get. The result was satisfactory. I might have been talking about an aspidistra for all the sign she gave. She wasn't concerned about plants. She had no suspicion she was part of one, a very elaborate one—that we all were. All she cared about was steering the conversation away from her room and what might be taking place there.

"You're very clever, aren't you, Dave?" she said smoothly. "And what happened to the girl?"

I looked at her for a moment longer. I needed very much to know what kind of a woman this really was, and I'd had enough of her acting. I had to shake her up a bit, for my own satisfaction.

"I'll show you what happened to the girl," I said, and her eyes widened slightly at the tone of my voice. I took the glass from her hand, set it on the floor, and placed mine carefully beside it. "This is what happened to that girl," I said, and I grabbed her and pulled her to me roughly. I heard her startled gasp. "Dave, please—"

Then I was kissing her hard and forcing her down on the bed. I guess I wanted to see if she'd panic, and for a moment I thought she had. There was a second or two of desperate resistance, or so I thought; then I heard something fall to the rug—two objects—and realized that she'd just been holding me off while she kicked off her shoes. She made a funny little triumphant sound in her throat and came to me as if she'd been waiting all her life for some man to realize she wasn't made of glass and wouldn't break—or as if she'd just been waiting all night for me to make the tactical mistake of laying rough hands on her.

I felt her fingernails dig through my shirt, and her mouth was warm and responsive despite my violence. I found my clever plans and sentimental reservations quickly becoming unimportant. I even found myself forgetting, more or less, that I was supposed to be a dedicated public servant on an important mission. I soothed my conscience with the thought that I wasn't really supposed to care what might be happening in her room. As a tough private eye, I was reacting the way I was supposed to. You might even say I was tending strictly to business.

There were those first frantic seconds—maybe minutes—of exploration and discovery; then we lay quite still in each other's arms, breathing hard. It was no time for jokes, perhaps, but suddenly I knew this woman well enough to try one even though I didn't know her at all.

"Here's your moment, Jenny O'Brien."

"Moment?"

"The critical moment," I whispered in her ear. "When you get it off with reasonable dignity. Don't forget the dignity. This I want to see."

She laughed softly, lying close to me. "Clothes!" she murmured. "Why do we have to wear them? Just pull it off me, darling. Skin me like a rabbit. Peel me like an eel, stockings and all."

"Do eels wear stockings?"

"Stop being silly and finish undressing me, damn you. You started it. You said the man liked to do the work. Dave?"

"Yes?"

"Do you love me?"

"Hell, no," I said. "I hate your lovely guts. Good God, talk about chastity belts. Where's the key to this thing?"

There were only the two of us in the world, talking breathlessly to bridge the awkward but necessary pause between promise and fulfillment. Then the roof of our private paradise fell in, the floor buckled, and the walls collapsed, leaving us exposed and unprotected, two rumpled strangers on a rumpled bed. What I mean is, somebody knocked on the door.

"Mummy," said a hesitant voice outside. "Mummy, are you in there? Mr. Clevenger, do you know where my mother is?"

15

Well, it wasn't quite as bad, I guess, as if it had never happened to me before. I'd been married once, myself. I'd had kids—they were growing up out West with the same mother but a different father—and I'd had a good chance to learn what it was like to have the most intimate moments interrupted by a small voice at the bedroom door. Still, it had been some years ago. I was no longer in the parental groove, so to speak.

"Oh, Christ!" I said, sitting up straight and wondering if I'd locked the door securely or if the kid was going to march right in on us. Then things began to add up—at least the possibility occurred to me that they might add up—and I drew a long breath and glanced at the woman lying on the bed beside me. "Congratulations," I said grimly. "That's real timing. You and that kid work well together, but she cut it pretty close, didn't she? Another couple of minutes and all would have been lost, as they say."

Jenny stared up at me. She looked pale and shaken,

and shocked at my suggestion. She protested: "Dave, you can't think I—"

There was another rap on the door. I said, "Call her off, will you? Tell her she doesn't have to break it down."

Jenny sat up and pushed back her rumpled hair. "Just a minute, darling," she called. Then she turned to me quickly. "Dave, I swear... oh, what's the use!" She looked around angrily, and called, "For God's sake, Penny, you don't have to wake the whole hotel! Let me get some clothes on, will you, darling?"

In spite of everything, I was a little startled. I guess I have old-fashioned notions about what the young are supposed to be told, and what they aren't. "Aren't you afraid you'll give her a trauma or something?" I asked.

"I thought your idea was that this was all planned between Penny and me," Jenny countered sharply. "And even if it wasn't, do you really think there's a modern teenager who doesn't know people go to bed together? What are we supposed to be doing in here, playing two-handed bridge? Get my dress, please." She spoke to my back as I got up. "Dave."

"Yes."

"You're wrong. You know you're wrong, don't you? I didn't plan it this way. I didn't... didn't even want it this way. If you don't believe me, come right back here. She can just stand there and hammer on the door and yell her damn little lungs out."

I glanced at her. "That's a hell of a maternal attitude."

"Motherhood, smotherhood. Even if I could do it to

you, do you think I could do it to myself? My God, I feel as if I'm going to fly into a million pieces!" She drew a ragged breath. "Well, I suppose we've got to find out what she wants. You haven't got a tranquilizer handy, have you?"

"Sure."

When I came back with it, Jenny was sitting on the edge of the bed with her face in her hands. She raised her head when I spoke to her, took the pill, and swallowed it with a little water. She gave me back the glass. After a moment she sighed, rose, and hitched various displaced lingerie straps back where they belonged, rather like a farmer snapping his galluses. Then she went through the standard feminine after-necking routine of settling her girdle, and smoothing her stockings up and her slip down.

She caught the garments I threw her and started putting them back on while I turned to wrap my tie around my neck, knot it and draw it tight like a hangman's noose. I guess it symbolized the way I felt I looked at myself in the mirror and scrubbed off some lipstick with a handkerchief. "Mummy, *please!*" said the voice outside the door.

Jenny said, "Oh, let the little monster in, Dave."

Parental tenderness wasn't exactly in the ascendant, I reflected. Well, it's only in the ads that everybody loves kids all the time. At the moment, I wasn't very fond of the brat myself. Nevertheless, I found myself somewhat abashed as I unlocked the door and let Penny enter to see the untidy bed and her mother standing by it, shoeless and disheveled, with unzipped dress and unbuttoned blouse.

It made things worse, somehow, that the girl was wearing flannel pajamas decorated with Disney-type bunnies: she looked about ten years old, although her hair was in curlers again, covered with a blue net nightcap thing that tied under the chin. She took in the scene gravely, glanced at me, and walked over to Jenny and started to fasten her up the back.

"You've got a run in your stocking, Mummy," she said tonelessly.

"I've got a run in my psyche, darling," her mother said. "I just snagged it on a stumbling-block named Penny. What's the big deal that couldn't wait until I got back to the room?"

"Oh!" Penny looked startled. Her reception here had apparently made her forget just what it was she'd come for. "It's... that man, Mummy," she said, glancing at me warily.

"Go on," Jenny said. "Mr. Clevenger, along with the rest of the U.S. government, knows all about Hans. Well, almost all. Go on."

It was no time to insist on my innocence of official connections. I just waited for Penny to speak.

"Well, he came with the instructions like he was supposed... Is it really all right to tell?"

Jenny made an impatient gesture. "Mr. Clevenger isn't a dope, darling. He's already guessed that I've been keeping him... distracted for a purpose."

Penny made a little grimace of distaste. "Some distraction!" she said. "Your hair looks like a hayrick after a hurricane, Mummy, dear." Her young voice was edged with scorn for these disgraceful grownup goings-on.

"Let's dispense with the comments on my appearance, Penny, darling. So Hans came on schedule."

"Yes. Mr. Ruyter came. He told me what... what you're supposed to know, what you're supposed to do. He was just about to leave when there was a knock on the door. Mr. Ruyter hid in the closet. I opened the door, pretending I'd been sound asleep. It was one of those two government men who've been following us—"

I asked, "The older one, Johnston?"

"No, the hairless one, the human skeleton." Penny didn't look my way as she answered my question. "He didn't believe me when I said I was alone. He must have seen Mr. Ruyter come in. I was... terribly scared, Mummy. He had a gun. He pushed his way in. I couldn't stop him. He started to search the room. When he had looked everywhere else, he pointed his gun at the closet door and told Mr. Ruyter to come out and..."

"And what happened?" snapped Jenny as the kid stopped talking.

"I don't know."

"What do you mean, you don't know?" I demanded.

"I simply don't know!" Penny protested. "Don't b-both of you jump on me like that! I d-don't know what happened." She sniffed and gulped, close to tears. "The government man wasn't looking at me. He was... very tense, telling Mr. Ruyter to come out with his hands up and not make any false moves. He wasn't paying me any attention. I just slipped out and ran here to tell you. That's all I know, except that they're still in our room. They haven't come out. I'd have seen them."

And there it was. Check to the gent with lipstick on his hanky and a silly look on his face. There was a lot of stuff here I didn't understand: there was still a question of just what kind of a person my freckled, passionate, vitriol lady was. I hadn't got much closer to solving that problem.

There was also a new slant on the mother-daughter relationship to be assimilated. I'd been taking the loving Penny-darling and Mummy-dear façade more or less for granted, but it had cracked a little tonight. Well, family life isn't always the pink lace valentine it's supposed to be; under the circumstances, some signs of strain could be expected. This hadn't surprised me as much as the various indications that Jenny had taken her young daughter into her confidence much more freely than I'd suspected, even to making the kid her accomplice in her dealings with Hans Ruyter.

But all this was unimportant beside the news that one of my special charges, one of my two cherished responsibilities, my handsome, girl-murdering baby, Ruyter himself, had gone and got himself trapped by a U.S. government agent.

Exactly what Larry Fenton thought he was doing wasn't clear. Unless he had much better connections among the local authorities than seemed likely, he was in no position, alone, to stage a legal arrest on foreign soil. On the other hand, he probably wasn't commissioned to deliberately remove Mr. Ruyter from the living and file him among the dead. Such commissions—contracts, they are called in underworld circles—are usually reserved for one government organization only, an organization to which he didn't belong and I did.

And if Larry had in mind just a quiet kidnaping followed by a quick trip across the border to the south, why had he picked the biggest hotel in the biggest city in Canada to close in on his quarry? A dark alley or country lane would have been more suitable. Probably Hans Ruyter had been counting on something like this when he took the risk of coming here tonight.

But this didn't really matter either. The grim fact staring me in the face was that Hans was in serious trouble. *He must not be harmed,* Mac had said. *They must get through... You will go as far as necessary.*

He had given me the blank check with his signature on it. It looked very much as if I was going to have to fill it in and cash it.

16

Jenny wasted no time wringing her hands or asking what to do—certainly she didn't ask me. The brief look she threw my way wasn't that of a lover, but of a fast-thinking woman trying to estimate the various factors of a troubled situation.

There was a quick, whispered conference between mother and daughter. Penny located a high-heeled white pump that had bounced under the bed, and set it beside one that hadn't. Jenny stepped into the shoes and headed for the door, patting her hair into some kind of order. The kid stayed at her side like a well-trained puppy. Both of them glanced around as I started to follow. There was a curious, hostile similarity between the two pairs of eyes, one with glasses and one without, that looked back at me coldly and dismissed me as an unfortunate nuisance nothing could be done about—but it occurred to me that some plausible explanation of my behavior would be required eventually.

Just getting Hans out of hock wasn't enough. I was going to have to make it look good to him and his female associate—not to mention Marcus Johnston, but that was something I'd worry about later. Maybe I could pull some strings by way of Washington and have Johnston called off if he started to present a real problem.

For the moment, my big concern was how to sell my rescue act—assuming I could carry it off—to the people most immediately concerned. I had to come up, fast, with a convincing reason why a presumably more or less patriotic citizen like Dave Clevenger would voluntarily involve himself on the wrong side of this international hassle—a reason that would finally impress my sincerity upon Jenny, who hadn't been impressed with my best efforts to date. I also had to convince Hans, himself, of my friendly and unofficial status, and he probably wasn't a man whose judgment would be clouded by gratitude, no matter what you did for him...

Jenny walked right up to the door of her room, started to look in her purse for the key, remembered she'd given it to Penny, and glanced at the kid, who shook her head. Jenny shrugged, and knocked. There was a moment of utter silence; then somebody turned the knob from inside and pulled the door open. Jenny marched right in, trailed by her daughter and, at a discreet distance, me.

It was a trite little scene inside; it could have been a still from a Grade B movie. Hans Ruyter, distinguished-looking in sports coat and slacks, lounged negligently by the closet door. At his feet lay a small automatic pistol, one of the Spanish jobs in which the barrel is exposed instead of being buried in the machinery as is the case with many American automatics, for instance the larger Colts.

The slim, naked barrel had been threaded for a silencer, which was in place. Whether Ruyter habitually carried his weapon that way, or whether he'd assembled it hastily in the darkness of the closet when he knew he was trapped, there was no telling.

It was a professional outfit, although the best pros don't rely upon firearms and prefer not to monkey with incriminating and illegal gadgets like silencers. Besides being embarrassing to have around if you're searched, they aren't as effective as they're cracked up to be, and that big cylinder screwed to the end of the barrel usually masks the sights and prevents you from shooting with any great accuracy.

The wicked little gun with its sneaky accessory told a lot about Hans Ruyter, professionally speaking—both good and bad. His attitude, however, was irreproachable. He looked self-confident and rather bored with the proceedings, which is the way for a prisoner to look, of course, even if he's scared silly. It makes the other guy wonder what he's got up his sleeve.

At the other side of the room, by the hall door, Larry Fenton was responding to the treatment by looking nervous and harassed. His gaunt face was shiny with sweat; even his shaved head showed beads of perspiration. He waved us past him left-handed, and used the same hand to close the door, being careful not to move his eyes or the gun—a sawed-off .38 revolver—very far from Ruyter.

Once inside, Jenny swung to face him. "Just what do you think you're doing in my room?" she demanded. "I don't care who you are, you've no right to break in here like this and frighten my daughter and threaten my… my friends! Now you just put that silly gun away and—"

Larry grimaced impatiently. "Shut up, lady."

"Well, I must say—"

"Don't."

Jenny opened her mouth angrily and closed it again. She was putting on a pretty good show, but I thought her attitude of high indignation just a little overdone. This was obviously the angle she and the kid had decided to play. What else they'd decided on, in their thirty-second council of war, remained to be seen. I was more interested in Larry at the moment. There had been shaky overtones in his voice when he first spoke, but he was gaining confidence. He risked a brief glance my way.

"I was hoping you'd come, Clevenger," he said, surprisingly. He seemed to have forgotten that we hadn't parted friends. He went on: "That's one reason I let the girl go… Oh, yes, I saw you sneaking out, honey, but I figured you were just going to get your mother, and maybe our detective here, and that's what I wanted. Now we're all here together, one big happy family… You can give me a hand with this handsome joker, Clevenger."

He was talking briskly enough now, but his eyes were kind of pleading. They were saying, as near as I could tell, that he'd apologize for hitting me, he'd do anything I wanted, once we were out of here, but there was no time for any of that personal stuff now. Right now we were allies in a room full of enemies, and he was counting on me to help.

I said, "You name it, amigo."

"First get his gun, there. Cover him for me while I get some information from the women... Careful, don't get between us. He's a real wise guy."

I refrained from pointing out that I'd been picking up wise guys' guns when he was still picking up rattles and putting them in his mouth and making happy gurgling noises, undoubtedly enchanting his proud young mother. Well, almost that long ago. I walked over cautiously and looked at Ruyter from a safe distance. Hans didn't move aside to let me reach the weapon by his shoe.

I said, "When I give the word, you'll move thirty-six inches to your left, or I'll kick you right between the legs. And if you move thirty-seven inches, I'll kick you twice and pistol-whip you with your own gun. Ready? *Shift!*"

I was aware of Jenny glaring at me, one protective arm about the kid in pajamas. To hell with her; she was only a minor worry now. While I was talking tough, with my back to Larry, I winked at Hans. He was my biggest concern. I had to get the message through to him, at least. Otherwise, thinking me an adversary, he might foul me up when the action started. They all might, but Ruyter was presumably the most experienced and dangerous. I saw his eyes widen very slightly. He hesitated. I made a threatening movement forward. He shrugged and stepped aside.

I picked up the silenced automatic, checked the loads, and in a sense there was really no further problem here. I had a reasonably quiet weapon in my hand. All I had to do was turn and fire. It was the only safe and certain way to handle a nervous man who also had a gun.

I knew it, and I knew that the coldblooded, treacherous move would take Larry completely by surprise, and I knew that Mac would approve it, or at least condone it. Anticipating some such situation, he'd as much as given me absolution in advance. The only thing I didn't know was the gun. It's only in the movies that you pick up a strange weapon belonging to someone else and shoot the pips from the ace of clubs at fifty paces. On the other hand, Ruyter was a pro, and his gun wasn't likely to be off enough to make much difference on a man-sized target at pointblank range…

I was stalling and I knew it. The ridiculous thing was, the stupid little dope trusted me. He'd punched me in the jaw, he'd kicked me in the ribs, and still he trusted me to forget personalities and behave like an All-American boy in this moment of crisis. It was crazy, it was infuriating, and still I couldn't quite bring myself to put a bullet into him like I should, either to disable or kill, as long as there was a reasonable possibility of accomplishing the same result by less drastic means.

After all, I told myself, it wasn't as if I had an old hand like Johnston to deal with. If I could just get close enough, I should be able to handle a shaky boy without damage. I let the weapon snap closed, and aimed it at Ruyter.

"Okay," I said to Larry without turning my head. "I've got this one covered, partner. I'll blow him in two if he gives me a dirty look."

I winked again. Hans responded with a microscopic nod, acknowledging my signal at last. I didn't kid myself we'd got ourselves much of a mutual-assistance pact, but at least he'd probably wait to see what help I could give, since I was offering it free. Facing him over the gun, I couldn't help remembering a dead girl in a motel bed, fifteen hundred miles back along the road, but that was personal and irrelevant. *He must not be harmed,* Mac had said.

"All right, Mrs. Drilling," Larry said behind me. "I want you in that chair over there."

I shifted position so I could watch and still keep Ruyter covered. It was a logical move, and it gained me a couple of feet, almost a yard, toward Larry. I saw Jenny move toward the indicated chair, hesitate, and sit down. Penny started over to join her.

"Not you, girlie," Larry said. "You come right over here, honey. Turn around. Turn your back to me. Now put your hands behind you."

He looked at us over her head: an odd, challenging, defiant look. Then, abruptly, he grabbed Penny's wrist and twisted it up between her shoulder blades. The kid cried out and went to her knees. Jenny gasped and started up from her chair, and sank back slowly, as Larry put his gun to Penny's head.

I made a sound of protest, and managed another step in

the right direction. "Look, fella, you can't just—"

"You keep out of this! Just watch the man like you were told. Don't interfere!" Larry's voice was sharp. "Now, Mrs. Drilling, there is something you have that we want, and we're tired of waiting for it. We're not going to let you get out of the country with it. You're going to pick it up somewhere—somewhere here in eastern Canada— and you're going to tell me where, or you're going to hear what a dislocated shoulder sounds like happening to your own kid. We're tired of being led around by the nose, Mrs. Drilling!"

Jenny licked her lips. Her face was pale under the freckles. "We?" she breathed. "Where is your associate? Does he know what you're doing?"

Something changed in Larry's eyes. "Never mind Mr. Johnston!" he said quickly. "Mr. Johnston is off having an important phone conference with Washington. I'm handling this *my* way."

Well, it wasn't the first time a young operative had taken a wild, independent gamble in the hope of looking good in his senior's absence. I gained another couple of inches his way, but it got me a quick, suspicious look that wasn't promising.

"Come on, Mrs. Drilling!" I didn't like the sound of his voice at all. He was right on the ragged edge; he was unpredictable and dangerous; he knew he had to pull this off all the way or be crucified when Johnston got back. He said shrilly, "Tell her what it feels like, honey! Tell your mom how it hurts!" He forced the kid's arm up farther.

Penny moaned. "Mummy, it hurts!" she gasped. "Mummy, tell him! *Please* tell… ahhh!"

I was looking for a clear, safe shot now. I'd made a mistake passing up the chance, earlier. Larry must have sensed some kind of a threat, because he threw another glance my way, and somehow he lost his grip on the kid's wrist while he was doing it, and she twisted around and threw her arms around his knees, and that, as they say, was when the egg hit the fan.

It all happened at once, they were all in motion very fast, and it all seemed very slow and inevitable. Hans reached for something in his pocket, and Larry looked that way while desperately trying to struggle free of Penny, who clung to him tightly. And Jenny was coming out of her chair and making a dive, not for Larry but for me—she hadn't got word that I was on the right side, or she hadn't believed it. Well, I'd been expecting something of the sort; it didn't catch me wholly by surprise.

Hans had whipped out a little package of cigarettes, but he didn't handle it like cigarettes. He pointed it like a gun at Larry, who'd used a knee on the kid to free himself. She was laid out on the rug, and he was taking aim at Hans with the .38, and I'd lost a fraction of a second sidestepping Jenny's flying tackle.

I'd still have made it, however, if I'd had my own gun, but Hans' clumsy, sightless rig shot as high as Benjamin Franklin's kite. I felt the recoil, and heard the more-or-less silenced cough, and saw plaster fly from the wall on a line well above Larry's head. I pulled far down and fired again, hastily, but the .38 went off before the Spanish job kicked back at me a second time. How Hans was making out with his camouflaged weapon, whatever it was, I didn't know and didn't care as long as he stayed alive, the way I was supposed to keep him by any means necessary—but when I looked at him, after making sure of Larry, he was sitting on the floor with a funny, surprised look on his face.

Larry's only shot had been very good, or very bad, depending on the viewpoint. There was a lot of blood on Hans' shirt, and he was obviously dying, and that was that.

17

I stood by the door for a full minute, listening. That was first on the priority list. If there had been anybody awake within range of the earsplitting crack of the .38, not to mention the double cough of the silenced automatic, we didn't have to worry about anything but cops. They'd take care of all our other worries.

On the other hand, if there was nobody around but sleeping hotel guests, we might just get away with it. A man wakened from a sound sleep by a single, confused stutter of sound can't always be sure just what woke him—not sure enough to do something about it in a strange hotel in a strange city, perhaps a strange country. There aren't too many tourists public-spirited enough to call the desk, or the police, to report some gunshots they aren't even sure they heard, knowing the red tape that's bound to follow.

Nothing moved in the hall. I gave it another couple of minutes by the watch, and the silence outside remained unbroken. Well, it was time I had a little luck on this job, for whatever good it could do me now. I drew a long breath and turned from the door, to meet Jenny's eyes. She was crouching on the rug in numb silence, exactly where she'd landed after trying to throw me for a loss. She was staring at me helplessly, perhaps because in that room I was the only other creature showing life.

It was kind of a shambles. Larry was dead almost at my feet, and a little distance away the kid lay sprawled in her pajamas, still out cold. I hoped it was no more than that. Across the room, Hans Ruyter sat against the wall with open eyes and a red shirtfront. I walked over to him. He'd finished dying while I checked the hall; he was as dead as he'd ever be. As far as I was concerned, it couldn't have happened to a nicer guy. I wasn't a bit sorry for him, only for myself.

I stood looking at him grimly, knowing that I'd made the one mistake that's inexcusable in my line of business: I'd let a mistaken humanitarian impulse louse up an assignment. I'd had strict orders to see that Ruyter got through at any cost. I'd known just how to do it, and I'd had the weapon to do it with, but I'd hesitated over paying the full price in blood. I'd tried to do a bargain job instead of the one I'd been assigned.

So two men were dead instead of one, and the job was shot to hell, and sooner or later I'd be back in Washington facing a couple of departmental psychiatrists who'd try to determine the full extent of the softening of the brain and whether or not the disease was curable—but that was kind of beside the point, at the moment. I squatted to examine the thing that looked like a cigarette package—a British brand called Players, if it matters—and saw the little hole out of which something lethal was supposed to come if you squeezed the right place the right way. It occurred to me that this, or something like it, could be the real answer to what had killed Greg, not the hypo left in Elaine's room.

I didn't monkey with the thing. I didn't know if it had been fired or not, and I didn't know how to fire it. It might even be booby-trapped in some way, and I'd made enough of a fool of myself for one night without winding up with a cyanide dart in the eye. But they certainly were a tricky bunch, with their acids and their silencers and their disguised blowguns.

I walked over to Larry. He had a hole in the head. In a sense, I reflected, he'd always had a hole in the head. It had just taken him a while to die from it. I felt nothing particular about his death, now, except regret that it hadn't happened on my first shot instead of my second. I looked at the crazy automatic I was still holding, and I looked at Jenny, still crouching there as if she was afraid to move. Maybe she was.

I said, "What the hell kind of loused-up weapons did your boyfriend carry, Irish? If his gun had shot straight, he'd be alive now. But this crummy thing shoots two feet high at four yards. I wouldn't have believed it if I hadn't seen it."

She was still staring at me, wide-eyed. Crouching

there on the rug, she was no longer the self-possessed woman to whom I'd recently almost made love: she was a scared girl. Well, death by violence isn't pleasant to see, particularly if you've never seen it before. I sensed that she hadn't.

She licked her lips. "But you... *you* shot a U.S. agent!" she breathed. "I thought... I don't understand..." She stopped, looked at me with vague suspicion, maybe hope, and said stiffly, "Another trick, Mr. Clevenger? Tell your friend to get up and wipe the catsup off his face."

"You tell him," I said.

She looked at Larry, obviously dead, and the hope—if it had been that—faded. I looked at the gun in my hand and saw some stuff hanging out of the silencer. Part of the sound-absorbent packing had been blasted loose by the two shots I'd fired. I examined the weapon more carefully, and saw that the whole silencer was cockeyed. Hans had either crossed the threads, screwing it on in the dark, or he'd bent it, dropping the gun at Larry's command. Not lining up properly, the silencer had thrown my shots way off. Maybe I owed Hans an apology. You could make a case for its not being his fault.

I took out my handkerchief, wiped the gun clean, and went over and put it into his hand, closing the dead fingers around it.

"What are you doing?" Jenny asked, behind me.

"They shot each other," I said. "They shot it out at point-blank range and both died. Very neat. Maybe the cops will buy it."

"But it isn't true," she said dully. "You shot him. The government man. I saw you." She frowned up at me, as if her thinking processes were slow and difficult. "Why?"

I'd had time to think it over after a fashion, and I said, "That's a goddamn silly question, Irish."

She licked her lips again. "What do you mean?"

I said, "All right, all right. So you didn't get me into bed and crawl all over me. So you didn't say you wanted a friend in your corner when the showdown came. Okay. Nobody's quoting you, are they? Who's throwing your words in your teeth? Not me."

She said, shocked, "You can't mean—"

"Cut it out," I said. "You're not responsible. Nobody's saying you are, are they? I killed him. Say I killed him because I didn't like the way he shaved his head. Say I killed him because he was twisting the kid's arm. Relax, Irish. I'm a big boy and I don't ask anybody to share the blame for what I do. I'm not asking you. But don't pretend you don't *know* why I did it, or I'll…" I stopped, and grimaced. "Ah, hell. It's a mess, anyway. It always is, when they break out the guns. That's why I leave mine home when I can. You'd better see about Penny. I'll get some water."

But her maternal instincts weren't operating yet. She was still staring at me in a horrified way. "But I never meant… I never asked you to *kill*…"

I said, "Sure, Irish. Sure. Don't brood about it. I'll figure a way out. Just give me a little time to think."

"But you *can't* have shot him just because I said—"

"I told you," I said. "I shot him because he was hurting the kid, and I'm a sucker for kids."

"When we first met, you said you hated the little creeps." She got up slowly, never taking her eyes from me. When I didn't speak, she went on breathlessly: "But it's mad! It's absolutely crazy! You can't think I ever meant for you to—"

I said, "Look, Irish, the guy is dead. See? Dead, like in corpse. Let's not waste any more time on who meant what. If I misinterpreted your desires, ma'am, I most humbly apologize. To you and to him. There really wasn't time for a consultation, if you'll recall. I just did my poor best, ma'am, and the next time you get in bed with a man, ma'am, and tell him you're doing it because you need his help, you'd better spell it out a little better or pick a guy who can read minds."

It wasn't a very nice line to take, I guess. Basically, it was the same cheap love-at-first-sight approach that Greg had probably tried, earlier. However, unlike Greg, I now had a dead body to lay at my feet to prove my sincere affection. The fact that she didn't seem to want it—either the body or the affection—didn't really matter.

She whispered, "I'm sorry. Really, I'm sorry. I had no idea anything like this would happen or I'd never…" She stopped, frowned at me, and said: "He was a government agent and you shot him! Does that mean that you're not… I mean, that you *weren't* working with him; that all the time you were really—"

"A poor damn private dick from Denver, named

Clevenger," I said. "Just like I always said, ma'am. And right now I'm a poor damn private dick named Clevenger on his way to the electric chair, if we don't get the hell out of here quick. She's your daughter, not mine. We'll just leave her lying there if you say so."

"Oh!"

She seemed to come awake at last, and she looked guiltily over at Penny, who was beginning to stir. Jenny hurried over, suddenly full of remorse and concern. I went to the bathroom for water; I couldn't help thinking bitterly that I'd finally made it. Now that it was too late, I'd made it: at last I had the woman fully believing in Dave Clevenger, the susceptible private eye with the ready trigger finger.

I heard the kid speak out there, and I called, "Is she okay?"

"Her glasses are broken and she's got a bruise on her chin," Jenny called back. "Otherwise I think she's all right. Aren't you, darling?"

Penny said something inaudible, in a fuzzy voice. I let the water run a bit to cool it. I heard the kid speak again, and something moved in my mind, and I remembered something I should have thought of before. I remembered the same young voice, in my room, asking if it was all right to tell. Jenny had said yes, and Penny had said that Hans—Mr. Ruyter, she'd called him primly—had told her certain things, just before Larry Fenton barged in. Some instructions had been passed along to the kid. It was a slim hope, but it was better than no hope at all.

But there was no time to go into it now, and this butcher shop was not the place for it. I had to get us space and time. I walked in with the glass of water and held it for the kid to drink.

"We've got to get out of here," I said. "We've got to get out without attracting attention. We won't check out. No luggage, no nothing. We just up and walk out. Understand?"

She hesitated, and started to look toward the two dead bodies, and restrained herself. "All right," she said stiffly. "All right, Dave. What do I do?"

"Well," I said, "you get the kid dressed just the way she was earlier this evening, hairdo and all. The assumption is she hasn't had her clothes off. And you fix that bird's nest on your head and put on a pair of nylons that don't look quite as much as if they'd been through a briarpatch. You can stick an extra pair in your purse if you like and a toothbrush for each of you, and that's all. When you come downstairs, you'll both look as if you were just continuing a long and pleasant evening by having your gentleman escort drive you around the lovely old city of Montreal."

"Where will you be?"

"I'll pick up a couple of things from my room, and go down and get the car from the garage and bring it around front. It will probably take me a quarter of an hour, but let's say thirty minutes to be sure." I glanced at my watch. "In exactly thirty minutes, you two come out the front door of the hotel, laughing and happy. I'll be waiting. You climb in merrily, and we'll be off. Okay?"

I went out, leaving them with the two dead men for company. Outside, I checked my watch again: twelve thirty-seven. I had some notion of hunting up a pay phone from which I could safely confess my sins to Washington, but it seemed more diplomatic to wait until I had more than a faint hope to report along with the blatant errors. Besides, I wasn't sure I could afford the time.

Maybe I was doing a lovely person a grave injustice, but I was fresh out of sentiment for the night, and I wasn't about to trust a woman just because I'd killed a man for her, or she thought I had. I went quickly to my room and used the phone there to order the Volkswagen made available. I looked around the room, stuck a couple of things in my pockets, grabbed my hat, and went out again, closing the door firmly enough to be heard by anybody listening nearby. I walked briskly past Jenny's door, turned the corner by the elevators, and pushed the button. The elevator came, opened with a metallic rumble, closed again, and went back down. I waited.

They were quick, I'll hand them that. I didn't know there was a lady alive who could change stockings and reconstruct a fancy modern hairdo in four minutes flat, nor had my boyhood experiences indicated that a fifteen-year-old maiden could even get a dress off the hanger, let alone put it on, in that length of time—but four minutes after the elevator doors had clanged shut, they were coming around the corner.

Jenny was in good shape. No one, looking at her, would guess that she'd seen love and death since dinner time. The kid wasn't fully assembled yet, but they were working on her. She was fixing her own hair while her mother zipped and buttoned her. They were so busy with the under-way grooming job that they didn't see me at once. Then they came to a sudden stop.

I was on again, as they say in the theater. I walked up to Jenny, looked at her for a moment in what I hoped was a bleak and disillusioned manner, and deliberately slapped her across the face.

"You cheap slut!" I said. "You lousy, teasing bitch! So you were going to run out and leave me holding the baby. The dead babies."

She glanced helplessly at the kid and back to me. "Dave, I—"

I reached into my pocket and took out my little knife, and flicked it open one-handed. There are easier ways of opening it, but that one impresses people.

I said, "I tried to do it nice, Irish. I didn't blame you for anything, did I? I didn't complain about the way you got me into this mess and then tried to weasel out of the responsibility when it came up murder. All I asked was that we stick together, work together, to get all of us clear together if it could be done—and the minute I step out the door, you're on your way without me, or trying!"

"Dave," she said. "Dave, please, I didn't mean—"

"You never mean," I said. "Who do you think you're playing games with, Irish, some little C.P.A. or professor of home economics? Mrs. Clevenger's boy David isn't about to face this rap alone. And if he's got to die for it,

he isn't going to die alone. The next time you step out
of line, I'll kill you. I hope I make myself clear, ma'am.
Now we'll all go down to the car together, smiling and
gay, and if anybody makes a wrong step or a wrong sound
there'll be a lot more blood on the hotel's rugs than there
is already. I don't like guns but I'm real sharp with knives.
That's a pun. Get moving, both of you."

It was, I thought, a pretty good speech for an off-the-
cuff effort. It seemed to go over well. They moved into
the elevator when it came, and they smiled and laughed
when I told them to, and we got out at the garage level,
and my car was waiting for us. Things were breaking my
way for a change.

Montreal is a big city, and it took me a while to work
my way out of it. I tried to get news on the Volkswagen's
radio, but all that came through on the local stations was
Canadian hillbilly music and rapid-fire announcing in
French, which is not my favorite language. This came too
fast and too accented for me to understand it. Once out
of town, however, the little Telefunken radio reached out
and got hold of some English I could follow, and I learned
that I wasn't the only one with troubles.

The world was still in a sad state, and airplanes were
still falling out of the sky like rain or hail, ships were
sinking, cars were crashing, trains were leaving the tracks
wholesale, and the U.S. Navy was still investigating the
recently announced loss of one of its pet atom subs. There
was some discussion of the fate of the *Thresher,* a similar
vessel that had met a similar fate some years earlier. At

least it had gone down and never come up, and I got the impression this was what had happened to the *Sculpin,* as the latest casualty was called. The weasel-worded reporting made it hard to be sure of even this word.

I drove along, listening and wondering. You're never told everything a job involves; and sometimes, as in this case, you're hardly told anything, but you can't help trying to connect it up with stuff you read in the papers and hear on the radio. I couldn't see what I could have to do with a missing submarine, but I didn't dismiss the possibility that there was a connection. Well, for the time being the admirals would have to worry about their sick tin fish alone; I had other things to think about.

The newscast ended without a mention of a double killing with international implications in a Montreal hotel. It was early yet, I reflected, but if Johnston should come looking for his missing partner we wouldn't have much of a lead, certainly not enough to do any driving in the wrong direction. I glimpsed an empty picnic area along the dark roadside ahead, and pulled in and stopped.

Jenny sat up and looked at me. I heard the kid stir in the cramped rear seat. After the display of team-work mother and daughter had put on tonight, I didn't like having either of them behind me, but there was a limit to the number of human bottoms that could reasonably be accommodated, for a long drive, upon the two small bucket seats in front.

"All right, ladies," I said. "Stage one has fired successfully and we're off the launching pad. Now it would be nice if somebody would tell me which way to go. I'd hate to set course for Mars if it's the moon we want." Nobody said anything. I looked at Jenny, whose face was a pale blur above the dim white of her blouse. I said, "Come on, Irish. Don't make me do a Larry."

"A Larry?"

"That was the given name of the dead guy back there, the arm-twisting Fenton character for whom I may be taking credit if this getaway doesn't work. Didn't you know?" She shook her head minutely. I said, "I don't just twist arms, doll. When I want an answer and don't get it, things can get very rough."

"What… what do you want to know?"

I said, "Well, right now I don't really want to *know* anything. I just want what I asked for, a direction. I want to get out of this country fast, and I think you people must have something lined up. Well, don't hog it. Your friend is dead; there's room for another." Nobody spoke. I said harshly, "Come on, now. North, east, south, west, or a point in between. Aim me the right way. Later you can tell me when to fire the retro-rockets." Jenny said nothing. I sighed. "All right, here we go again. Penny, let's get out of the car where I can take off my coat and roll up my sleeves. I know you probably feel like a human punching bag already, honey, and I'm real sorry, but your mother's gone and lost her tongue again…"

I heard the kid stir in the darkness. "Oh, Mummy, for heaven's sake *tell* him!" she gasped. "Don't let him… I can't *stand* any more tonight. Just tell him. *Please* tell him!"

Jenny drew a long, rough breath and said, "Northeast, Mr. Clevenger. Follow the St. Lawrence past Quebec City but stay on the south bank. Drive to a place called Riviere-du-Loup, then turn right toward Fredericton." There was a little pause, then she said savagely: "That should keep you busy for a while. I hope it makes you very happy!"

"Sure," I said, and it did. Not that I really needed the direction—I already knew where she had to go, remember, and she'd actually pointed us the right way—but the fact that she could be bluffed into giving it promised well for the future.

18

Mac said, "I don't know, Eric. What are you trying to say, that Ruyter wasn't as important to the operation as we've been assuming?"

"Something like that, sir. Not essential, anyway."

It sounded weak, like a schoolboy saying it wasn't a very big window he'd broken and it had been cracked anyway. Mac was silent. I could visualize him frowning, some five hundred miles to the south and west of where I stood in a little red roadside phone booth. We'd passed the longitude of Washington a day earlier. We'd come a long way, in more ways than one.

"It seems unlikely," Mac said at last. "After all, our information is that he was the man sent from overseas to do the White Falls job. The woman is only a convenient tool he picked up when he got there."

I looked out through the glass at the convenient tool sitting in the Volkswagen parked nearby. It was still dark but I could see that mother and daughter were taking advantage of my absence from the car to hold a conference, of which I flattered myself I was probably one subject. I would have liked to know the others.

I said, "I'm not sure we've been given the right dope on this situation, sir. I've got a hunch there's an element our informants overlooked, somewhere. In particular, I don't think they had this woman figured right."

"In what way, Eric?"

"She was supposed to have been doing all this because she was crazy about Ruyter, wasn't she? Well, I can testify that she has displayed no visible signs of infatuation, sir. I got a distinct impression that while she'd tolerated him as a bed partner a few times, more or less to spite her husband, she didn't even think that much of him any longer. At one point she came damn close to asking me to help her escape from his clutches, or words to that effect. When he was shot, far from mourning over his body, she seemed a lot more concerned over Larry Fenton's death—well, over the fact that a government man had got killed."

"If passion isn't the lady's motive power, what alternative do you suggest?"

I hesitated. "Well, I think he had something on her, sir. Something big enough that she *had* to jump when he cracked the whip. Bigger, say, than a spot of casual adultery."

Mac said, "The man is dead. He is cracking no whips. And still you seem to think there's hope that she intends to carry his plans to completion."

"Yes, sir," I said. "That's the impression I get. Maybe

the whip has been passed to someone else, someone here in the east. But even if it hasn't, even if the possibilities of blackmail—if that's what it was—died with Ruyter, what choice does she have now? She's committed; she can't turn back. What's behind her except an embittered husband, a lot of law, and four dead bodies? She may not be legally responsible for all of them, maybe not for any of them, but once she's caught up in the investigation she'll never get free and she knows it. There's also a little charge of dealing with her country's enemies, technically known as treason. She can't stop now."

"You're assuming she has somewhere to go."

"Hell, she was going there when I stopped her in the hotel corridor, sir. I'm sure Ruyter had an international escape hatch up here somewhere; and he told the daughter enough before he died that mama thinks she can find it, or at least make contact with someone who'll lead her to it." I paused briefly. "Do we have any dope on how Ruyter got here in the first place? I mean, did he come by plane, or ship, or did he swim ashore like a seal? If we knew how he was landed, maybe we'd know more about how he was expecting to get away."

Mac said, "It's a reasonable thought. It occurred to me some time ago."

"And?"

"And the people who have that information are not parting with it, Eric. Security is very tight in this area."

I made a face at the telephone box on the wall. "One day we're going to get so damn secure that the Russians will take us over and nobody'll know it because nobody'll dare talk to anybody else, about that or anything else." I drew a long breath and played my lone ace. "Well, you go ask these secure people if the name Gaston Muir means anything to them, sir. He lives in a place called French Harbor. He has a boat there. According to my map, French Harbor is a small coastal village on Cape Breton Isle, Nova Scotia, not more than thirty miles from our ex-mining town of Inverness. I just got that out of the kid. I'm getting to be a terrible bully, sir."

"Gaston Muir," Mac said. "French Harbor. I'll see what reaction it brings. This is what Ruyter told the little girl?"

I said, "If you call a teenager a little girl, you're apt to get a poke in the eye, sir. But, yes, if she's telling the truth, and I think she is up to a point, this is the dope Ruyter wanted Penny to pass on to her mother. Mrs. Drilling was to come to French Harbor properly equipped—I presume this means with the papers. She was supposed to make contact with either Ruyter himself or this Muir character at a certain waterfront joint at six o'clock in the evening the day after tomorrow—well, that's tomorrow, now. In case of emergency, say if she couldn't make it, she was supposed to get word to Muir by way of the general store; leaving a certain innocuous message. The kid wouldn't tell me the code. She balked there, and I figured I'd got enough for the time being without getting really rough."

"I see. Tomorrow evening, you say?"

"Yes, sir."

"And you think Mrs. Drilling will go through with it in spite of the changed situation?"

"I think she has no choice, sir. And in order to buy her way to safety, she's got to bring the papers as instructed. Ruyter's friends may possibly help her get away without Ruyter, but not without the stuff. She's got to have something to bargain with." I paused for breath. "What it amounts to, sir, is that we've lost one of our carrier pigeons, but with a little luck the message may still get delivered if we can all stay out of jail until tomorrow night. That's up to you. I've got some seven-eight hundred miles still to go, and I'm not going to be able to do much hiding and dodging if I'm to stick to Ruyter's timetable. Nor am I in any position to outrun the Canadian cops, with forty horsepower and two lady passengers. Somebody's damn well got to tell them to look the other way as we go by."

There was a little silence. I didn't venture to guess which way he'd decide. Even if he thought there was a chance of retrieving the mission, he might feel that the fumble-witted agent on the spot was just too damn incompetent to take advantage of it—and he'd have a point.

He said at last, "It will take a good deal of delicate diplomatic maneuvering to arrange a safe-conduct for you through three provinces, Eric, when the charge is murder. I don't really know if it can be done, without causing disastrous comment."

I said, "They shot each other, Fenton and Ruyter. At least I set it up that way. The authorities don't have to believe it, but they can pretend they do for a day or two. That way they're only looking for some missing witnesses. They don't have to look too hard."

"And how do you propose to handle a certain Mr. Johnston, who is presumably on the vengeance trail, or will soon be?"

"You handle him, sir. Have somebody call him off. For questioning about his partner's death, say."

"I can only make suggestions and recommendations. I have no authority over his department."

"No, sir."

"If I should fail in my efforts to have him withdrawn—"

I waited a little and said, "Yes, sir?"

"I hope you have no tender, brotherly feelings for the gentleman, such as you seem to have had for his youthful associate."

"No, sir."

"There is also the little girl—excuse me, the young lady. She may prove to be a nuisance. Since you do not seem to understand indirect orders, Eric, I will give them to you directly: if she, or anyone else, should again threaten the success of this mission, you will arrange for them to have an immediate accident, preferably fatal. Do I make myself perfectly clear?"

I said, "Yes, sir."

He went on: "We were not assigned to this job to be nice to little girls, or to clumsy young operatives from other bureaus; quite the contrary. Being nice to people is not our business. If you simply have to be nice, Eric, I will refer you to a very pleasant gentleman who recruits for the Peace Corps. You're a little over the age, I believe, but I will be glad to give you the highest recommendations. Maybe they will make an exception for you, since you obviously have the good of all humanity at heart."

"Yes, sir."

"That's all. I'll see what can be done at this end."

"Yes, sir."

I heard the connection being broken. I let my breath out softly. Well, I'd had it coming. And he was letting me go on, and even backing me, and I've been reamed out before. It could have been worse. But I still took off my hat and dried my forehead with my handkerchief as I went back to the car.

I made kind of a production of it, in fact. My harem, suddenly busy with comb and lipstick—you wouldn't have known they'd said a word to each other all the time I was gone—looked at me questioningly as I got in, still mopping my brow.

I said, "Phew. That was my boss in Denver. The F.B.I. has already been at him. He's washing his hands of me, he says. He wants no part of murder, particularly a murder tied in with something as big as this. That's the way he put it." I looked at Jenny in the semi-darkness. "What the hell have you got me into, Irish?" She didn't speak, and I said, "Well, whatever it is, you're going to get me out, hear? Clear out of the country. The kid's already told us where to go. French Harbor. But you're the girl who's going to tell us where to pick up our steamboat tickets. Right now."

Jenny licked her lips. "What do you mean?"

I said, "Don't act dumb, doll. Everybody's after something, something big, and you've got it or know where it is. Well, I want it. Your pal Ruyter had a getaway all arranged, but his friends aren't going to be happy about smuggling a stranger out of the country. Only, they aren't going to get what they want unless they do, understand? Because you're going to give it to me, not to them."

"Are you... are you threatening me, Dave?"

I laughed. "Cut it out, doll. I gave you a chance to play it smooth and nice—chivalry, romance, and the works— and you tried to run out. Now we're just two crooks on the lam, and I'm lots bigger than you, and lots tougher. And if you don't think I can learn every last thing you know, just try me." I grimaced. "Take my word for it. Now or half an hour from now, you'll talk. I didn't become a private op because I had a weak stomach, and my life's at stake. You can talk in one piece or you can talk all busted up. That's the choice."

The kid spoke from the back seat. "He means it, Mummy! You know he means it! Tell him!"

Jenny said, "Dave, do you know what it is you're asking for?"

I said, "No, and I don't give a damn. Just so it's valuable enough to somebody that they'll help me out of this mess you've got me into, and maybe throw in a little cash on the side."

"It's... some scientific information about a certain project of my husband's, a very secret U.S. government project."

"So what?" I laughed sharply. "Irish, you're not going to get on the patriotism kick at this late date? Jeez, look who's talking!"

She was silent. I waited. The kid stirred in back but didn't speak. Jenny drew a long breath and said, "Inverness."

It was no time to be hasty. I was David Clevenger. I wouldn't know where a lousy little mining town in Nova Scotia was located. Matt Helm might, but not Dave Clevenger. I got out a road map, reached up to switch on the dome light by my left ear, and checked the index.

"Inverness, J-6," I said. "Here we are, just down the coast from French Harbor. Irish, you might even be telling the truth. Where in Inverness?"

She hesitated only briefly. "The post office."

"I see. You mailed it to yourself. Bright girl. Under what name?" She paused again, and I said irritably, "Don't make me do my tough act all over again, damn it! Haven't I convinced you I mean it?"

Jenny glanced at the girl in the back seat, as if for advice or, maybe, moral support. Penny said quickly, "Go on, Mummy! Please tell him. After all, we're all in this together, aren't we? We need his car and his help to get there, don't we?"

Jenny sighed. "Oberon," she said. "Mrs. Ann Oberon."

"Sure," I said softly. "Sure. Sorry I had to talk so nasty. Mrs. Ann Oberon. Inverness. Nova Scotia." Well, it was part of the public record now. I was free to use it as I pleased. I drew a long breath and looked around at the kid.

Now that it was all over, I was embarrassed to see that she looked a bit mussed; I'd had to shake her up some, earlier. I said, "And my apologies to you, too, Miss Drilling." She looked back at me with naked, serious eyes. I didn't think I was her hero any longer, even if I had licked two bad men with only a little stick to help me. That was a long time ago. I said, "You're in a bad way without those glasses, aren't you, honey? Let me see them. Maybe I can stick them back together temporarily."

She gripped her purse tightly and shook her head. She wasn't taking any favors from me. She knew I was just trying to salve my conscience by being nice to her. I took the purse from her fingers and got the glasses out. They weren't badly broken. A hinge had been twisted loose in her struggle with Fenton, that was all. I tightened the remaining screws with the point of my knife, and reinforced the corner with adhesive tape from a box of Bandaids I had in the glove compartment. Then I picked up my handkerchief and checked the lenses, to see if I'd got any smears on them.

The car was very still. Nobody moved. I looked through the lenses, and remembered a pair of glasses I'd examined in their trailer, a pair of little-girl glasses with a very strong prescription. These were not the same lenses. They weren't even close. In fact, they had no prescription at all. They were just colorless sunglasses.

19

Somebody moved at last. In the back seat, the kid brought a hand up from behind her. She was pointing something at my head. This much I knew without really looking around. Sooner or later I was going to have to turn and see just what she was threatening me with—if I got to live that long—but it seemed best to take a moment or two first to try to straighten out my scrambled thoughts.

I looked at the useless glasses in my hand. Penelope Drilling was nearsighted. This much was firmly established. When you came right down to it, it was just about all that was firmly established about her. Crazy as it might seem, nobody had ever made a real identification of the kid for me, and I doubted anybody had for Greg. As I recalled Mac's statement on the subject, the camp had been pointed out to Greg when he came on the job—just the camp. And shortly before that mother and daughter had spent a day unobserved in the mountains of British Columbia while the man who was supposed to watch them was having trouble with his low-slung Detroit glamor-buggy.

Apparently nobody had really checked that the two people who'd come down from that mountain lake had been the same two people who'd gone up. That was the only reasonable explanation I could think of for the evidence in my hand. After all, who looked at kids, anyway, on a job like this? To an adult agent concentrating on the behavior of the senior female Drilling after her temporary disappearance, one junior miss tagging along with spectacles on her nose and braces on her teeth would look pretty much like any other from a distance, particularly if she kept doing the same odd teenage stunts with her hair.

It was very clever and tricky, like the rest of this operation, and when I had time to work it all out I'd undoubtedly find that it cleared up a lot of problems that had bothered me—about Jenny's behavior, for instance— but first I had to survive the next few minutes.

I said carefully, in a puzzled voice, "That's funny. I thought—"

"What did you think, Mr. Clevenger?" It was the kid's voice, and still it wasn't. It had a cold, adult quality that no fifteen-year-old girl could ever achieve. "Don't move," it said. "Don't even look around."

"I said, "Honey, if that's a gun you're pointing at my head, go easy. I'm a mouse. I'm a little woolly lamb. You don't want to hurt me."

"What did you think, Mr. Clevenger?"

"Well, I was told that Penelope Drilling was nearsighted to the extent of eight or ten diopters, if that's the right way to put it. Anyway, she's pretty damn nearsighted,"

"And?"

"Well," I said, "I came on the job kind of hastily, remember? After Mike Green had turned up dead, I was just sent out to make contact with a woman and a young girl associated with a certain truck-trailer combo. Color, make, license plates. Thumbnail sketch of subject. These spectacles are windowpanes, honey. As a detective, I have to conclude that either they're not yours, or you're not Penelope Drilling."

"You put it very clearly, Mr. Clevenger. I'm not Penelope Drilling."

I drew a cautious breath. At least I'd got her to say it out loud and I wasn't dead yet. I shook my head ruefully.

"You must have had lots of fun laughing at me behind my back. And your so-called mother, here, who's she?" I didn't look at Jenny. "Do the freckles come off, too?"

"No." The kid's voice was scornful. "No, Mummy-dear is quite genuine, aren't you, Mummy-dear? But the real Penny-darling is being held in a safe place out west as a hostage for Mummy-dear's good behavior. Ugh. You may turn your head now, Mr. Clevenger."

I guess I should have felt smart. After all, I'd just said blackmail to Mac, on no more than a hunch, and blackmail it was. I turned slowly and looked at the weapon she was holding less than a foot from my face. This didn't make me feel smart, because I'd seen it before in the trailer, in a drawer of toys—seen it and passed it by without interest. It was a child's water pistol made of transparent plastic. That was the first impression. On closer examination— and I was plenty close—I could see that the supposed plastic was actually glass. The gadget was actually a cunningly made and ingeniously disguised syringe. The handle or grip was full of colorless liquid, and a little bead of the stuff had formed at the tiny orifice in what would have been the muzzle, had it been a real gun.

The kid said, "If I squeeze this trigger, Mr. Clevenger, you will never see again."

I said, "Sure, honey, sure. Just go easy. A guy without eyes isn't going to drive you very far." I shook my head wonderingly. "So that's what happened to Mike Green. Is it out of line to ask why?"

"Mr. Green had wandering hands," the cold young voice said. "Even very juvenile females were not safe from Mr. Green's casual, seemingly accidental, attentions. One day Mr. Green's exploring hands discovered… well, shall we say, indications that the child he thought to be Penelope Drilling was abnormally well-developed for her age, although she generally took pains to conceal the fact. At first the discovery merely intrigued him; then it made him think. Thinking, for Mr. Green, was a slow process, but I could see where it was leading him."

I glanced at the small, rather pretty white face, strange without the glasses and the innocent, childlike expression I'd come to know.

"Just how old are you, anyway?" I asked.

"I'm a little over twenty, Mr. Clevenger. Not that it's any of your business."

"And you left a glove behind in Mike's motel room that didn't belong to you."

She made a wry face. "As a measure of self-protection. I thought it was a reasonable precaution, but Hans was very angry. He said it was an error that could jeopardize the whole mission. He took steps to rectify it."

I said, "Yeah. I heard about those steps. Have you got a name?"

"You can call me Naomi."

"Naomi," I said. "Very pretty. One question, Naomi."

"Yes, Mr. Clevenger?"

"Why are you pointing that thing at me?"

That shook her a little. She blinked and said, "Why, I couldn't be sure how you'd react."

"How did you think I'd react?"

"I thought… well, that you'd be angry because of the way you'd been fooled."

I said, "Okay, I'll be angry tomorrow, or some other day when my conscience hurts me about the kid I was supposed to protect. That I never even got to see. Right now I'm tickled pink. Hell, I thought I was going to have to go clear to Nova Scotia and find this Gaston Muir character to make a deal about getting out of the country."

She hesitated. "And now you think you can make your deal with me?"

"Why, sure," I said. "With Ruyter gone, you're running this show, aren't you? I don't see anybody else in the picture, aside from this Muir, and I gather all he really does is run a boat."

"Yes, I'm running the show," Naomi said coolly. "And I may be dense, but I fail to see what you have to deal with, Mr. Clevenger. We've known all along the town where the documents are waiting; we told Mummy-dear to send them there. All I didn't know was the name of the fictitious person to whom they are addressed—she held out on us to that extent—but you've just given it to me. Thank you very much, Mr. Clevenger, and thank you in advance for the use of your car, and now if you and Mummy-dear will just get out… Keep your hands in sight, Mr. Clevenger!"

"Hell, I was just putting my hanky away… Okay, okay. Be careful with that damn thing!" I faced her over the back of the seat. "Listen, you can't just leave us here…"

I had the handkerchief ready. I shoved it up against the muzzle of the acid-gun, and got her wrist with my left hand, in a way that made her fingers open before she realized what was happening. Then I reversed the weapon and aimed it at her left-handed. She stared at me wordlessly, with hate in her eyes.

"Stay still if you want to stay pretty!" I snapped. "Irish!"

"Yes?"

I flung the damp handkerchief away from me, out of the car. I thought I could feel the flesh peeling from my hand, but it could be just imagination. I didn't take my eyes off Naomi.

"On the double, Irish. Take the keys, open the trunk—

up front, remember. There's a two-gallon canteen full of water. Come around to my side and rinse off my hand, real quick."

I stuck my hand out the open window and waited until I could feel cold water running over it. I still seemed to have four fingers and a thumb.

"I think I've got it all off," Jenny said. "I don't think you got much on you. The handkerchief must have caught most of it."

I brought my hand back inside, under the light. A glance told me she was right. There wasn't even a blister visible. I looked at the girl in the back seat.

"Does that metal scaffolding come off your teeth?" I asked. She nodded silently. I said, "Well, take it off, then. Let's see what you really look like."

She put her hands to her mouth and worked for a moment, and took them down. She was really quite attractive, in a diminutive, fragile way. Well, so is a coral snake. I remembered what Greg had looked like after she'd got through with him. It occurred to me that Hans Ruyter's death might not have been entirely due to inefficiency on her part. He'd bawled her out; he was the boss. Now he was dead and she was the boss. Perhaps she had wanted it to happen that way. I didn't put it past her.

I said, "Let us reconsider, doll. Would you still say I have nothing to deal with?"

She looked at me for a moment, and at the glass gun I held. Then she smiled slowly. "You are a very resourceful man, Mr. Clevenger."

"I can be a very useful man," I said. "I want out of the country. A little money would come in handy, too, but I won't be greedy about it. Do we have a deal, Naomi?" I heard Jenny, still standing outside the car, give an indignant little gasp of surprise and protest. To hell with her. She'd made her contribution. It was between the kid and me now.

Naomi's smile widened. "We have a deal… Dave."

I did one of the hardest things I've done in my life. I turned the vicious acid pistol around once more and gave it back to her butt first.

20

Jenny and I waited in the car outside the lone general store in a small town named after some saint or other. I suppose it was a kind of loyalty test. If we waited obediently where Naomi had put us, we proved one thing. If we drove off and left her, we proved something else, and she'd get on the phone and prepare a suitable reception for us at the Nova Scotia end of the line. She might do that anyway. In fact, I didn't think there was much chance she wouldn't.

Waiting, I amused myself by reading the various metal signs nailed up around the place. It was better than, for instance, worrying about cops and corpses and what Mac might or might not have been able to accomplish in the way of clearing trail for us. If anything can make Madison Avenue's cigarette and soft-drink slogans seem even cornier, it's being translated literally into French. Jenny stirred beside me.

"Dave."

"What is it, Irish?"

"You're not really going to... I mean, you can't possibly trust her!"

I glanced at my companion. She looked pretty good for having spent a hectic night in her clothes—well, mostly in her clothes. She looked attractive and resilient and, for an amateur, reasonably competent. It was a relief not to have to think of her in connection with a jug of acid. It was an association that had never seemed very plausible.

I told myself that mother love excused, or at least explained, most of her far-out behavior to date. I even considered trying to enlist her as a working ally. Acting together, systematically, we were much more likely to get the job done and get out alive afterward, than if we struggled along independently, hoping for individual breaks.

I was tempted. There's always the risk, in the business, that you'll get so damn wary and smart and suspicious that you won't take a chance on anybody, not even when it may mean the difference between failure and success. It was a mistake I didn't want to make here. On the other hand, I had my orders. Security was paramount. I was not allowed to take anybody into my confidence; I couldn't tell Jenny enough of the truth to sound convincing and persuasive after everything that had happened. And there was a conflict of interest. She was presumably concerned most of all with the safety of her daughter, while I had strict instructions to strangle any young girls who got in my way.

I said, as Clevenger, "Have I got a choice? Who else is going to get me out of this now? You?"

"She's a vicious, sadistic little monster," Jenny said. "You don't know what it's been like, driving with her all that way, living with her, pretending to be her *mother,* for God's sake! If I had a child like that, I'd dump it out of the crib and squash it underfoot! Like a tarantula!"

"Sure," I said. "What's the story on Penny, the real Penny?"

Jenny's expression changed. "They're holding her somewhere, somewhere out where we were a couple of weeks back. A mean-looking, farmer-type couple took her away. That's all I know. I could go crazy thinking about it, Dave. She's kind of a sensitive kid. Not a typical teenager at all. A shy, bright, studious fifteen-year-old, not really very pretty but awfully sweet. I suppose I should have left her home, as you keep saying, but my husband... well, it takes a special kind of man to make a reasonable home for a child all by himself. I knew Howard wouldn't even try. He'd be too busy with his light rays. I thought she'd be better off with me." Jenny moved her shoulders jerkily. "The way it turned out, I guess I was wrong. I was brought up too civilized. I didn't expect all this violence. Dave?"

"Yes."

"Will you try to help? Hans was supposed to call long distance after I'd turned over the papers and... and he'd made sure they were okay. He was supposed to call and have Penny set free. Naomi knows how to get in touch with them back there. Maybe you can persuade her... Oh, hell, here comes the little bitch now. What do you bet she didn't get anything for me to wear, just for herself."

Jenny hesitated, seemed to go through a mental struggle, and said very quickly in a low voice, "Dave, there's something you'd better know. Don't count too much on what we'll find in Inverness."

I looked at her, startled. "What the hell do you mean by that?"

She shook her head. She was watching Naomi approach, carrying a big package, looking like a sweet little thing in the morning sunshine, with her plain blue jumper and ruffled blouse and piled-up hair. Jenny whispered, "There isn't time now... Just be careful. There, I've done you a favor. You will try to help Penny, won't you?"

"I'll try."

I spoke mechanically. I was wondering what she was holding back that could louse us up. If, after all this, the stuff wasn't waiting in the Inverness post office, or if there was something wrong with it... well, I could worry about that when it happened. The present had enough worries without my borrowing from the future. I leaned forward so Naomi could squeeze into the back seat of the Volkswagen.

"Do you know they don't have any jeans in this forsaken country?" she asked brightly. "Why, it's practically subversive. All right, Dave, let's go. Stop in the first patch of woods. I want to get out of this droopy teenage outfit before I'm picked up for playing hooky from junior high."

She sounded brisk and cheerful. You'd never know, listening to her, that she'd committed murder and had a few other crimes in mind. I drove out of town and found a track running down into a stand of pines and stopped when we were out of sight of the highway.

"Your dressing room, ma'am," I said, and got out so she could tilt the seat forward. She reached back for her package and straightened up beside me.

"Come with me, Dave. I want to talk with you."

"Sure."

"Take the keys. We wouldn't want Mummy-dear driving a car all by herself. She might hurt herself."

I took the keys and followed Naomi. She moved off a little ways but stopped where we could still see, and be seen from, the car. She put her package on the ground and turned her back to me.

"I'm told you're a great button-and-zipper man. Demonstrate."

"Always happy to oblige."

I got to work on the familiar fastenings, reflecting that I was getting in a rut. If I wasn't bullying them for information, I was helping them take their damn clothes off.

"I'll just bet you're happy." Naomi's voice was tart. "Is she any good in bed?"

"Who, Jenny? You never gave me a chance to find out!"

"She's an awful pill, really. She was going to chicken out, you know. But Hans was way ahead of her. He never really expected her to go through with it all the way, voluntarily. That's why he had me ready to step into the kid's shoes, so he'd have something on Mummy-dear that would keep her in line until we got out of the country."

She pulled her dress and blouse off her shoulders and let them drop at her feet. Then she kicked off her shoes, peeled off her stockings, whipped her slip off over her head, and stood before me in nothing but a little pantie-girdle and a very tight, flat brassiere.

"Unhook me," she said, and when I'd done so she pulled the brassiere off and threw it as far as she could, and drew a long breath, turning to face me. "God, it's nice to breathe again. And eat. Did you ever try chewing a steak with a mouth full of stainless steel? There's another bra in the package. Get it out for me, will you? The next brat I impersonate, I hope she won't be so damn flat chested. Dave."

"Yes?"

"Do you like it?"

"What?"

"What you see, stupid!" She laughed. "What I mean is, we can have a lot of fun together, but first we've got to get rid of Mummy-dear. I mean, once we've made sure she isn't playing any tricks. I called Gaston Muir from that store back there. I told him to expect two passengers on his boat. Just two."

It was no time to act shocked or high-principled. And it was no time to act curious about where the proposed boat ride might end. I merely shrugged.

"Very cozy," I said. "Just so it's the right two passengers, doll. Don't *you* try any tricks. I wasn't born yesterday."

She smiled up at me approvingly. "What a suspicious

tall man it is! Don't worry, darling. We're going to have a swell time together. We'll have a million kicks, a million laughs. Hand me that shirt, will you?"

I handed her a dark print shirt and a pair of tight black pants and she put on a pair of sandals all by herself and we went back to the car where Jenny was sitting with a disinterested, disdainful look on her pretty, freckled, adult face, that was supposed to tell us she hadn't even noticed the striptease that had been performed under her nose, and mine. Fourteen hours later we were in Inverness, having stopped for no policemen—we'd hardly seen any; I wondered if Mac had somehow managed to get them clear off the roads—and for nothing else, either, except food and gas.

21

It was as easy as... well, as getting mail from General Delivery usually is. First, of course, we had to wait hours for the post office to open next morning, but once that ordeal was over, it was a breeze. There wasn't even anybody in line ahead of us. Jenny went up to the window, gave the fictitious name to the clerk, and turned back to us holding a big manila envelope bound with heavy cord. We closed in on her, Naomi and I, and escorted her back to the car. Naomi snatched the envelope and scrambled into the back seat.

"I saw a pay phone back on the main street by the gas station," she said breathlessly. "Drive us there while I see what Mummy-dear has for us. Damn. She's got it all tied up with string like she was afraid it would jump out and run away. Lend me your knife, Dave."

"To hell with you, doll," I said, driving. "You want my knife, you know how to get it. First you call in six strong friends to help you. You keep your toy gun. I'll keep my knife."

She made an impatient sound. "All right, *you* open it, damn you!"

I parked the car by the phone booth, took the envelope, cut the strings, and slit it open for her. She grabbed it back and pulled out the papers far enough for a look. I heard her breath go out in a long sigh of satisfaction as she saw the big red stamp on the top sheet. I could only read the one glaring word SECRET from where I sat, but I found it a great relief.

Jenny said quietly. "There's a policeman."

We looked up. An unmistakable officer of the law was strolling up the main street toward us. He wasn't a local cop, but a member of the Royal Canadian Mounted Police—in riding breeches, no less. I didn't see a horse. He didn't seem to be looking for any murderers or seeing any. Behind me, I heard Naomi stuff the documents hastily back into the envelope.

"What are you waiting for?" she breathed. "Drive!"

"Don't be silly," I said. "You want us all to spit on him as we go by, so he'll be sure to notice us? He's just getting a bite to eat. Go make your phone call."

The Mountie turned into a restaurant a block away. Naomi drew a shaky breath, squeezed out of the car, and entered the phone booth, clutching her envelope. When she was busy talking, I glanced at Jenny, beside me.

"Okay, Irish," I said. "What was that all about? That scare talk you gave me back while she was buying clothes?"

Jenny shook her head quickly. "Never mind," she

breathed. "It's all right. Whom do you think she's calling?"

"A gent called Gaston Muir, I presume," I said. "But don't ask me what I think she's telling him. I could be wrong, and I wouldn't want to slander a sweet girl by mistake." Jenny glanced at me, studied my face for a moment, but did not speak. Then Naomi was coming back to the car. I leaned forward to let her in.

"Drive on up the coast," she said. "I'll tell you where to turn."

I said, "I thought we were all set to make contact tonight in a restaurant in French Harbor."

She wasn't a very good actress. She met my eyes too candidly. "The plans have been changed," she said. "I got hold of Gaston and told him we already had the stuff. He can't get away immediately, he's got something to do with the boat, but he wants to meet us early this afternoon and make arrangements; in the meantime we're to go to a certain place and stay out of sight. I've got the directions."

"Sure."

The ocean was to our left as we came out of town. Well, actually the map said we were looking at the Gulf of St. Lawrence, and that the real ocean was way off to the north and east past the end of land, but it was enough salt water to impress an innocent New Mexico lad. Jenny drew a long breath, beside me.

"It's beautiful," she said, "but kind of scary. I always wonder what's out there under the surface."

"Fishes," I said. "And dead men's bones."

"Watch where you're driving," Naomi said behind me.

"Don't turn here. We stay on the pavement for another couple of miles."

We followed the pavement past a bunch of deserted coal mines, and then we followed the gravel for a way, and then we were on dirt, and finally we wound up at another mine way out in the woods. It looked like any little old mine, east or west. I suppose an expert can tell at a glance what came out of them, but to me they all look alike, whether they once produced gold, silver, copper, or coal. There are the same dumps, the same wandering rusty tracks that once made sense to somebody, the same picturesque, crumbling hoists and elevators, and the same weathered shacks.

At least they look the same to me, and I always have the same thought when I see one: *Now, there's a hell of a fine place to hide a body.* Apparently it was a thought that had occurred to other people as well, unless I was doing Naomi and her unseen friend a grave injustice.

I had no real doubt about what we'd been brought here for, Jenny and I. The trouble was, there wasn't much I could do about it. The message still had to be delivered, and I was running out of carrier pigeons. Hans was dead. Jenny no longer qualified. That left only Naomi to carry the ball—Naomi, and Gaston Muir, an unknown quantity. My sense of self-preservation is as strong as anybody's, but we're not hired, after all, just to stay alive, although it's considered a reasonable secondary objective.

My primary objective, however, was to get the stuff onto Gaston Muir's boat. In order to accomplish this, I had to keep both Naomi and her accomplice unhurt and unsuspicious, and the only safe way was to sit where I was put and wait for somebody to lower the boom on me. It took them a long time to get around to it. I suppose they were waiting, among other things, for me to get bored and sleepy. I considered dozing off, but decided it would be out of character. Jenny, however, curled up in the car and went to sleep.

Then Naomi started to chatter brightly about one thing and another, and then, sitting on a log, I heard him coming up behind me. I found myself hoping he was a better sailor than he was a woodsman, or that boat would never get out of the harbor. I saw Jenny stir uneasily and come awake and look our way and see him—both car doors were open for ventilation—but she was, thank God, too late to call a warning. A gun-barrel touched the back of my head before she could open her mouth.

Muir, if it was Muir, had a deep voice. "Do not move, Mr. Clevenger," he said, behind me. He spoke to Naomi: "You said he had a knife, girl. Get it. Then go watch the woman."

I started at the touch of the gun, as if he'd taken me completely by surprise. Naomi darted forward, and got the little folding knife from my pocket and backed off, looking like the kitten that ate the robin, pleased and proud.

She pocketed the knife, produced her glass pistol, slipped a rubber cap or stopper of some kind off the muzzle, and moved where she could aim the thing at Jenny.

The situation was self-explanatory, and as a reasonably bright agent I'd have accepted the fact that I'd been double-crossed, and we could have gone on from there, skipping the corny dialogue. But I wasn't supposed to be a reasonably bright agent, I was supposed to be a reasonably dumb private detective, so I went through the motions of looking shocked and outraged.

"Hey, what is this?" I demanded. "Give me back my knife. Naomi, tell your pal he's making a mistake—"

Naomi laughed. "The mistake is yours, darling."

"Why, you treacherous little bitch!"

I made as if to lunge for her and tear her to pieces with my bare hands. It was very dramatic, and I was told to sit still or get shot, and I sat still and went through the you-can't-do-this-to-me routine, and the I'll-get-you-if-it's-the-last-thing-I-do routine, and a couple of the other verbal gambits people are accustomed to perpetrate on TV when they have guns pointed at them unexpectedly. I mean, there's a whole literature on the subject, all of which assumes that the hero is an unstable idiot who's got to blow his top noisily every time his fellow-men, or women, prove unworthy of his childlike trust.

The man with the gun had moved around to where I could see him. He was a big, dark, middle-aged man with something of a belly on him. He was wearing a black seaman's cap, an old black suitcoat, a work shirt buttoned to the neck, and clean overalls. His gun was a Luger, old and worn but showing no rust or neglect. It was the first 7.65mm Luger I'd seen in a long time. You hear more about the heavier 9mm cartridge these days, but the 7.65 was once considered very modern and high-speed stuff, shooting a light bullet at well over a thousand feet a second when that was very rapid indeed for a pistol.

Gaston Muir, in contrast to his weapon, had a deliberate, slow-moving, almost gentle air. He let me rave a reasonable length of time, which was promising. I mean, if I'd been him, I'd have rapped me hard along the head with the gun-barrel to shut me up, but apparently he was a more kindly type. Maybe he even had objections to violence. It was an encouraging thought, but I didn't put too much stock in it. After all, he did have a gun.

"That is enough, Mr. Clevenger," he said at last. "I said, that is enough, man!"

I said, "Just do me one favor, Muir, if that's who you are?"

"I am Muir," he said. "What is the favor?"

I glared at Naomi. "Just let me get my hands on that slut for sixty seconds—"

Muir said, "Please, Mr. Clevenger. We sympathize with your disillusionment, but as a sensible person you must realize that there is no place for you beyond this point. If we were to take you farther, you would learn things you should not know. Now go over and join the lady, if you please."

I rose from my log, growling something blasphemous, and went over to stand beside Jenny, who'd got out of the car. She glanced at me, and looked at Muir, and licked her lips.

"What… what are you going to do with us?"

I was annoyed at her for asking. I mean, if he admitted frankly that he was going to take us into the mine and shoot and bury us where no one was likely to dig us up accidentally, what had we gained? And if he said he wasn't, how could we believe him? So why waste breath on a question that had only profitless answers, when the real answer was probably only a few steps and a few minutes away?

I guess I was really annoyed with her because, after almost two full nights and days in the same dress, she looked kind of wilted and wrinkled, as well as scared, and I was sorry for her. I didn't want to be sorry for her. I'd been sorry for Larry Fenton, and it had got me nothing but trouble. I reminded myself that Genevieve Drilling had bought chips in this game long before I had; there was no reason why she shouldn't stick around to see the last hand with the rest of us.

Naomi said, "What do you *think* we're going to do with you, Mummy-dear? You see that black hole in the hillside up there? Start climbing!" She waved her weapon at both of us. "You, too, Dave, darling."

Muir asked, "Where are the papers, girl?"

"On the back seat of the car."

"Are the keys in the car?"

"I think so."

"Make sure," Muir said. "And then get the coal oil lantern and the coil of rope that's in that shack over there. Behind the door. And put that un-Christian weapon away. There's no need for it here."

It was a frustrating situation. Usually, at the end of a job, you're closing in on somebody you're trying to catch. If you've used yourself as bait, which happens, at least there's a point at which you're allowed to stop acting meek and stupid: you can shed your shackles and start swinging. But here there was nobody to catch. In fact, my job was to see that they stayed uncaught, by me or anybody else.

There was nothing for me to do, therefore, but scramble obediently up the slope behind Jenny. If I should overpower my captor and his small female ally, I'd have to get right to work and figure out a way to let them escape convincingly, unharmed. It was simpler and safer—at least as far as the job was concerned—just to play it docile and hope that the gods, or Gaston Muir, would be merciful. I wasn't silly enough to count on mercy from Naomi.

She came scrambling up the dump behind us, with a coil of rope over one shoulder, swinging a kerosene lantern by the bail. I noticed that, regardless of Muir's orders, she hadn't put her trick gun away. Jenny came to a stop at the mouth of the mine, breathing hard. It had been a hard climb up the slope of loose rock, particularly in high heels, and her face was shiny and the thin white stuff of her blouse clung damply to her arms. Her eyes were big and dark. She looked at me as I came up, with a question in her eyes, but the others reached us before she could put it into words.

Gaston Muir had to light the lantern, since Naomi was too young to have learned about the methods of illumination that preceded universal electricity. Muir gave it back to her burning, and relieved her of the rope. No seaman can ever take a coil of rope without doing something with it; and we stood waiting while he re-coiled it more neatly.

Naomi made an impatient sound. "Just what's that for, anyway?" she demanded.

Muir looked surprised at the question. "Why, we have to tie them up, girl. We have to give ourselves time. I sent the preliminary signal this morning right after you called, but our friends will not come in all the way until they receive confirmation. They do not like being close to land. We must give ourselves time to make the final transmission and then reach the rendezvous point off shore, without interference."

Naomi was frowning. "You mean," she said, "you mean you're not going to kill them?"

There was a little silence. Muir looked at her, and started to speak, and changed his mind. He seemed actually embarrassed. He looped the rope carefully over his arm, and gestured toward the mine opening, and cleared his throat.

"You go ahead with the lantern," he said. He cleared his throat again, and went on, "Killing is not my business, girl. I just transmit signals and run a boat. For some years I have run one here. Soon I will be running one somewhere else, wherever they send me. I try to run it without unnecessary bloodshed. Killing is not necessary here, so we will not kill."

"But it *is* necessary!" Naomi said hotly. "You know perfectly well, if they get loose too soon, they can spoil everything. We don't have to take that risk! Besides... besides, they know too much about me. I'll never be able to come back to this continent if they're left alive to talk."

Muir was studying her thoughtfully. "Why," he said, "why, you *want* to kill, don't you? Do you know what Hans Ruyter said about you over the telephone? He said you were vicious, ambitious, and unreliable. Just what did happen to Hans, girl? How did he come to die? There will be questions asked about that, you may be sure." His voice did not change as he continued: "Be careful with that weapon. I am a very good shot, and one can deliver the documents as well as two."

Naomi's pretty baby face showed a moment of ugly, adult fury, quickly controlled. She shrugged her small shoulders and turned away. Muir gestured to me to follow. I guess it was a compliment: it showed he considered me the more dangerous of his two prisoners. He didn't want me too close.

"No tricks, Mr. Clevenger," he said. "As you have heard, no one will be hurt if you both behave."

"Not hurt!" cried Jenny. "Tied up way underground? Why, we'll die there before anybody finds us."

Muir said, "I doubt that, Mrs. Drilling. Your tall friend looks like a resourceful man. I'm sure that in time he'll manage to get you both free. Now follow him, if you please."

She hung back. "But you *can't*—"

"Go on!" he snapped, losing patience, and she was silent. I heard her enter the tunnel behind me.

It wasn't a nice place. I mean, I have no spelunking ambitions whatever. I don't like being underground, even in the best-run tourist caverns, and this was just an old, neglected, downward-sloping hole in the side of the hill. It was plenty wide enough, but a bump on the head quickly taught me it had not been cut for men six feet and above. There were rusty rails underfoot, laid on rotting wooden ties. From time to time we passed a corroded pulley or a twisted hunk of cable or a snarl of broken wire.

I didn't like it, but in a way it was a relief to know that the job was practically done. All we had to do now was let ourselves be tied up like docile children, and hope that Muir's slow sanity would continue to control Naomi's homicidal impulses. After the two of them had departed to take the papers on the final stage of the long journey that had started on the other side of the continent, we could worry about getting free. As Muir had suggested, I had some resources, including a trick belt buckle constructed specifically for taking care of ropes with which I might be tied.

The tunnel got lower, in one place so low that Naomi, ahead, had to crouch well down to pass under the down-hanging rock. Her black pants were dusty now, I noticed, and her shirt tail was out. Coming to the same place, I had to get down to all fours to make it through. On the other side, the tunnel widened and there was plenty of headroom again.

Behind me, I heard Jenny complaining bitterly about her impractical, hampering clothes and the damage she couldn't keep them from sustaining in these rough and dusty surroundings. I had time to think that her griping had a contrived sound, as if she was talking to make reassuring noises, on the theory that any lady whose mind was on her nylons couldn't possibly be considered dangerous…

As the thought hit me, I turned, but I was too late. The fool woman had already gone into action. Maybe she really thought she was taking a last long chance for her life. Muir must have got careless, listening to her whining complaints. When he hunched down to make it under the low place, his gun was out ahead of him, and she was ready. There was a quick scuffle and a cry:

"I've got his gun, Dave! Here, you know how to use it!"

Then the Luger came sliding down the tunnel toward me. I'd as soon have been presented with a live rattlesnake. I didn't want to shoot anybody. Jenny was on top of Muir, hammering at him with her fists in a vigorous and unladylike manner—I remembered her telling me about all the trucks and tractors she'd driven as a girl. I wondered where the hell all the nice little movie heroines had got to, the ones that cower against the wall, whimpering, while the men fight it out. In this spot, wanting nothing but peace and quiet and some ropes

around my wrists and ankles, I had to have a redheaded
Irish wildcat on my side.

But there was no time for heavy thinking. I came out
of my temporary daze. The gun was there and I snatched
it up and threw myself aside, figuring there was bound to
be acid in the air in a moment. I rolled over once and hit
the side of the tunnel and came up with the gun ready, and
saw that I was more or less right.

Naomi had set the lantern down. Ignoring me, she was
starting to draw a bead with her vitriol gun on the violent,
thrashing struggle taking place on the old mine tracks
above her. Apparently she didn't care which combatant
she sprayed, just so she got a piece of the action.

It couldn't be permitted, of course. I mean, to put it
bluntly, Jenny was expendable, but Muir wasn't. He had
to, by God, run a boat, and he was going to need good
eyesight to do it. I wasn't about to have him doused with
acid, no matter what happened to anybody else. He'd
given me the cue. He'd indicated that one could deliver
the papers as well as two—if that one was Gaston Muir.

I tried to do it the easy way, however. I honestly tried. I
aimed the Luger to disarm, not to kill. I just kind of forgot
what it was Naomi was holding. She'd swung her weapon
high and now she was bringing it down, cowboy-fashion.
They all think they have to chop holes in the air to aim a
gun, forgetting that this up-and-down business only made
sense back in the old cap-and-ball days when you had
a fired percussion cap to toss clear, between shots, so it
wouldn't jam the action.

As once before on this job, I had a snap shot to make with a strange pistol, but Muir's gun was a nicely balanced piece that shot where it was pointed, and I made it. The little high-velocity 7.65mm bullet intercepted the kid's swinging hand in midair, and the acid-gun blew up six inches in front of her face. I mean, when a glass container full of liquid is hit by a bullet traveling that fast, things don't just shatter, they explode.

There was a moment of complete silence, broken only by a kind of trickling sound as dirt dribbled from the tunnel roof here and there, dislodged by the concussion of the Luger. Jenny stopped trying to tear Muir to pieces and he stopped trying to fight her off. Everybody seemed to be waiting for something. Then Naomi screamed.

22

It was a fairly horrible sound in that underground tunnel; it seemed to fill the place with madly chattering and whimpering echoes. Naomi screamed again, and turned toward me blindly. One sleeve and shoulder of her dark cotton shirt was splashed with lighter stains where the acid was already taking out the color. She had both hands to her face. She didn't seem to know that one was bleeding, drilled through by the same bullet that had destroyed her weapon. She stumbled over the lantern and fell, and the light went out.

She was screaming steadily now, but that wasn't the sound that interested me. I mean, in the absence of water to wash the stuff off with, or morphine to kill the pain, there was really nothing to be done for her. She was just another carrier pigeon out of the running—maybe I should say flying—and I concentrated on the little undercurrent of noise that told me that Muir, like a sensible man who'd lost his gun, was getting the hell out of there. I prayed that nothing would get in his way, and that he'd be real careful and not break a leg, or something, getting down the slope to the Volkswagen, and that the car would start for him...

Naomi had got turned around somehow and was moving away, stumbling, falling, and screaming in a mechanical, keening way like a badly wounded animal. I heard her begin to crawl. She seemed to be heading downhill, farther underground. After a while I could no longer hear the scuffling sounds of her progress. After a while, the screaming, too, stopped. The silence that followed lasted several minutes. I was in no hurry to break it by moving. I wanted Muir to have all the time he needed to get away.

"Dave."

I had almost forgotten about Battling Jenny, my unwelcome savior. "Right here, Irish," I said.

"Do you... do you think she's dead?"

"That stuff doesn't kill," I said. "You just wish it would. Hold everything while I make a light."

I struck a match and found the overturned lantern, unbroken. Some kerosene had leaked out, but there was still plenty in the cistern. When I got it lit again, the yellow light seemed very bright compared with the utter darkness that had preceded it. There were dark splashes of liquid, and shards of broken glass, on the floor of the tunnel. Avoiding these, I made my way up to Jenny, who was sitting where the roof came down low. Her heroic battle for our lives and liberties had left her rather picturesquely disheveled, but at the moment her damage seemed relatively insignificant.

"Come on," I said, getting down to negotiate the low bridge.

"But... but you can't just *leave* her down here!" Jenny's voice was shocked.

I drew a long breath. It wasn't her fault, I told myself. She'd done what she thought best. Maybe I should have taken her into my confidence earlier, orders or no orders.

I said, "For reasons I'm not at liberty to divulge, Irish, I am more interested in our boy Muir right now. I hope he knows how to drive a Volks. If not, I suppose I'll have to show him."

The hell of it was, he didn't. When we emerged from the tunnel, the car was still down there and he was in it trying to figure out where the Black Forest elves had hidden reverse gear. Then he looked up and saw us and slammed the lever into low, ran the car up the steep slope a little way, and let gravity roll it back while he spun the steering wheel frantically. Another uphill charge and rollback, and he had the bug turned around far enough that he could make a jolting circle back into the forest road. I took out the Luger, aimed carefully well clear of him, and fired twice for effect. I wouldn't have wanted him to get the idea I wasn't real mad at him for stealing my car.

When I looked around, after setting the safety again and putting the gun away, Jenny was watching me with a curious, speculative expression on her dirty face.

"You... you wanted him to get away," she said uncertainly. "Didn't you?"

I regarded her for a moment. She was really pretty spectacular. "Turn around," I said.

She looked a little surprised, but turned. I went through the zipper-and-button routine for the third or fourth time—I guess by actual count the third—and she stripped off the trailing, grimy remnants of her blouse. She bent over to rip away some rags and loops of lingerie stuff hanging down below her dress while I fastened her up again. The linen jumper wasn't clean and it was kind of bare of top, but at least it was reasonably intact.

Straightening up, she said as if there had been no pause, "You did. And you let him capture you on purpose, didn't you? I wondered, when I woke up and saw you sitting there pretending not to hear him behind you... Who are you really, Dave? What are you trying to do?"

I said, "If you'd peel that nylon fuzz off your legs, you'd look almost respectable."

She said, "If it hadn't been for that government man you killed in Montreal, I'd still think you were one of them." She stopped. Her face turned a little pale under the dust and freckles. She said, "That's it isn't it? You *are* one of them. I was right about you all along. I just didn't understand what you wanted. I thought you were all just setting an elaborate trap for Hans. But that's it! My God! You'd go *that* far to make it look... you *wanted* those papers to go out of the country. That's been your job all along. To get them out without anybody's knowing that...

that they were *supposed* to go out. Oh, my God!"

I wasn't supposed to admit anything, but she sounded distressed and the stuff was on its way at last and I couldn't help saying, "What's the matter?"

She looked at me without speaking for a second or two. Then she said, "There's nothing in that envelope."

I stared at her. I remembered a warning she'd given me, and later more or less retracted. I wanted to grab her and shake her, but I managed to keep my hands to myself.

I heard myself say, "Come again, Irish?"

"There's nothing in it, I tell you! Nothing of any importance to anyone."

"But I saw—"

"You saw a top sheet with a big red stamp. That's all you saw. If you'd looked underneath, you'd have found nothing but some dull correspondence of my husband's. I warned you twice, Dave. Way back there in Montreal I told you I was a perfectly ordinary person. Not clever. Not sinister. Not the kind of person who'd betray her country. But you insisted on believing I was subtle and wicked. The only one I've ever betrayed, if you want to use the word, is Howard; and I wouldn't have done that if he'd just... well, never mind *that*!"

I said, "But you did take his briefcase."

"Certainly I took his damn briefcase! The way he waved it under my nose, how could I help taking it?" She drew a long breath. "The way they all acted, you'd think treason was like syphilis and you caught it in bed. Just because... because I'd got myself a bit involved with a man who turned out to be a spy, did that mean I'd necessarily taken leave of my senses? When I learned what Hans was and what he really wanted, I called the F.B.I. Of course I called anonymously. I didn't want it all over the project. I just wanted to get rid of him. He was getting that way, too. I mean, he seemed to think that just because I was willing to sleep with him, I'd steal for him—as if the two things had anything to do with each other!"

Well, it was a new slant on the situation. I said, "So it was you who called time on Ruyter. I guess I was told something about that."

"What else could I do? I suppose I should have rent my garments and poured ashes on my head and gone in to the security people to make confession, or something, but it didn't seem necessary." She'd sat down to roll wrecked stockings to the ankles; she didn't look at me. "But my God, the way they watched me after Hans was gone! And then I got his phone call. It was too ridiculous even to get angry at. As if I'd rifle my husband's desk and go chasing off into Canada for *him*—I mean, the man had delusions of grandeur!"

I said, "But on the record, that's just about what you did do, Irish."

She grimaced. "Damn them, they drove me to it! They made me so mad! They couldn't ask me! Do you understand? They never came up and said, please, Mrs. Drilling, will you cooperate? Will you help us set a trap for this man—that's all I thought they were after. But no, I'd breathed some subversive air, I was contaminated,

I couldn't be trusted. So they tried to be clever. And Howard, my own husband, helped them. Can you imagine how *that* made me feel? There he was with his damn briefcase, telling me how important it was, practically shoving it into my hands. I realized that he really expected me to steal it. They all did. They were counting on it." She looked up at last. "So I stole it, Dave. I stole it, and took it out to the garage, and took out everything marked secret or confidential, and shoved it all down into a big bag of garden fertilizer, except the top sheet. I knew Howard would never look there. He can't stand the smell of it. It's mostly dry sheep manure."

"And then you made up an envelope and stuffed it with the single cover sheet clipped to some correspondence you'd found in the briefcase, and mailed it to yourself here, like Hans had told you on the phone."

She said, "Of course. If they were going to play games, I'd play games. I'd lead them around by their long snooping noses, and then at the right moment I'd laugh at them and tell them where their priceless phony documents really were—they were phony, weren't they? I mean, they surely wouldn't have let me near any real ones. And then I'd go off with Penny and find a place to live where nobody's ever heard the word security. Only... only, when I got to Hans, up in Canada, it turned out it wasn't a game after all. I was stuck with it. All I could do was stall and hope something would happen before my little trick came to light." She drew a long, shaky breath. "I'm sorry, Dave. I guess it was an irresponsible, childish thing to do, but I just got so mad I had to do *something*. I mean, using my own husband to entrap me, for God's sake! I hope I haven't ruined everything for you."

I thought of three dead men and a dead girl, not to mention another girl who wasn't quite dead—at least I didn't think she was. Then I thought about a continent three thousand miles wide and jet planes flying at so and so many miles per hour, and telephones, and radios, and all the other marvels of modern science. And suppose we got the right stuff out here—by rocket, perhaps—how would we go about getting it into the right hands now? It was too late for a new deal. We'd just have to play the cards we had, or let them play themselves.

I said, "Let's just see how the stick floats, as the old mountain men used to say. Why don't you see if you can find a brook to wash your face in, while I pay a visit to a sick friend?"

Jenny looked startled. "Oh! I'd almost forgotten—" She glanced at the black mouth of the mine with distaste. "Is there really anything we can do for her now? Wouldn't it be better just to get help here fast?"

I said, "It's not a question of what we can do for her, Irish. It's a question of what she can do for us. And nobody invited you."

She was bright enough to catch my meaning. She said quickly, "Don't be silly. Just let me dump some dirt out of my shoes so I'll have room for more."

The mine didn't bother me this time. I had nothing else left to do; I might as well be crawling through the bowels of the earth looking for something I didn't particularly want to find. The first thing I found, beyond the point where the shooting had occurred, was a scrap of acid-stained cloth caught on a nail. The next thing was my own knife. It lay at the side of the tunnel, unopened. It had blood and stuff on it as if it had been handled before being dropped.

I didn't ask myself what Naomi had been wanting with a knife. I just wiped it on my shirt tail and dropped it into my pocket. Below were more signs of her progress. Finally, I found her. She was lying face down between the rusty rails, small, torn, dusty, and motionless, but I could hear her painful breathing.

If you can do it, you'd damn well better be able to look at it. I put the lantern down and turned her over gently. I heard Jenny gasp and turn away, gagging. Well, I'd seen it once before; I'd known what to expect. I guess you could say Greg was avenged. I found her good hand and checked her pulse, for no very sensible reason. After all, if she could breathe, she was alive. The small hand I was holding closed on mine.

"Dave?"

The voice was strange and kind of thick. It seemed to come from deep down and far away. I said, "That's who."

"Kill me," the voice said.

I said, "Sure. Just hang on while I find a suitable rock. Do you prefer having your brains bashed out from front or rear?"

"I mean it. You did this to me. Well, finish it. Kill me."

"Take it easy, doll."

She clung to my hand. "Don't let them save me! Don't let them take me to a hospital and… and wash me off and transfuse me and… I saw what it did to Mike Green. I don't want to live like that. I'd be a freak, a blind, faceless freak with a claw for a hand. Kill me!"

"Sure," I said. "Sure, doll. But it will cost you."

I heard Jenny draw in her breath sharply. Naomi said pleadingly, "It hurts, Dave! God, how it hurts!" I didn't say anything. She spoke in a different voice, almost businesslike: "What do you want?"

"Information," I said. "Penelope Drilling. Where's she being held? Who's holding her?"

Naomi whispered, "You'd blackmail me for *that*, damn you, after what you've already done to me?"

I started to rise. "So long, baby. I'll send the doctors out when I get to town. They'll take good care of you."

She gripped my hand tightly. "I love you, Clevenger. You're almost as mean as I am."

"Meaner," I said. "I'll come visit you in the hospital. See how you're coming with your lefthanded Braille."

I heard Jenny stir behind me. I guess she thought I was terrible, even though it was her child I was fighting for. She didn't count here. She didn't know how it was. She wasn't a pro, like the two of us.

Naomi laughed harshly. "You're a darling," she gasped. "You're a wonderful, coldblooded beast. There isn't a drop of sympathy in you, is there?"

"Not a drop."

"I couldn't stand sympathy. That's another reason why… they'd be full of sympathy, all the kookie doctors and nurses. What do they know? Who wants their damn sympathy? Try a town called Greenwich. Greenwich, British Columbia. The home is about three miles west of town. A little farm. The brat's there if she's still alive. That I can't guarantee. The name on the mailbox is Turley. Mr. and Mrs. Claude Turley. Okay?"

"Okay," I said. "I've got a pill for you. Just a minute while I get at it."

"Oh, one of those," she breathed. "I had one, but I dropped it back there and couldn't find it again. Then I tried your knife but I couldn't get it open one-handed."

"It takes practice," I said. "Here you are. You know the drill. Get it between your teeth and bite down. If you really want it."

She said softly, "Chicken. You're going to make me decide, so you can tell yourself it wasn't you who did it." I said, "Hell, I'll cut your throat if you want me to, doll. But this way's clean and painless, they tell me."

"Give it to me. It's beginning to hurt again. I can't stand much more."

"Open your mouth," I said.

"So long," she whispered. "I hope you have nightmares about me. In Technicolor. Give it to me now."

When we came out of the mine, into the fading sunlight, a police car was just nosing into the opening below us where the Volkswagen had been and was no longer. A man got out of the rear and came up toward us as we slid and scrambled down the dump. I had him pegged right away. He was wearing a green tweed suit. I don't know why it is, whenever they get out of the uniform of the day, tweed is what they always get into, real rough and hairy and colorful.

"Mr. Helm?" he said as I reached him. "I'm Commander Howland, U.S. Naval Intelligence. I'm working with the Canadians on this. I want to congratulate you. It looks very much as if our fish is taking the bait. Come on, I guess you deserve to be in at the kill."

23

It was a high bluff overlooking the ocean. The sun was down, but inshore you could still see wicked underwater rocks lurking beneath the innocent-looking surface. Farther out, the sea was dark and impenetrable. Way out there, a white boat was heading diagonally offshore, leaving a V-shaped wake.

"He's still holding on," said Commander Howland. "I guess he hasn't bothered to open the envelope. Or maybe he'd keep on anyway, to get away. So Mrs. Drilling switched papers on us?"

"So she says."

"It's a pity. We had some very pretty ones fixed up by some of the best scientific brains in the world. It would be ironic if a handful of old letters turned the trick just as well." Howland put his eye to the tripod-mounted telescope behind which he was lying. It was a massive glass, looking like an overgrown half-binocular, with an objective lens as big as two fists. Howland said, "As it seems to be doing.

Course, approximately due north. Speed, about twenty knots. He's got the old bucket up to maximum hull speed now; look at the way she's squatting. You know he put a new engine in her last year, a big one. They all figure if they double the horsepower they'll double the speed, but it doesn't work like that. All those extra horses just gave him about three knots more than he had with the old mill. The tub wasn't built to go faster."

I said, "You seem to know quite a bit about Muir, sir." In the business, we make a practice of sirring all officers above the rank of major or lieutenant commander. It makes for good working relations with the service brass.

"We've been watching him for three years, just in case we might have need of him or the people he contacts from time to time. It was merely a question of getting him something big enough that he'd feel justified in arranging a rendezvous." Howland rose. "Take a look if you like. I'm going over to talk with our friends. Sorry I can't invite you. The less you learn about the technical end of this, the less you'll have to forget."

"Sure."

I watched him go over to a knot of uniformed men stationed farther down the bluff. They had some radio stuff set up, and I couldn't have cared less about the technical details. I was, however, just a bit curious about whom all the communications gear were supposed to talk to, but I didn't expect to be told and I never was. I got down behind the low telescope and put my eye to the ocular and got things focused. The boat came in sharp and clear as if in broad daylight. It was quite a glass.

I lay alone, watching Muir's little vessel buck the waves out there, smashing them into sheets of flying spray. Jenny was gone. This was all too highly classified for her to witness; besides, she wanted to be handy to learn what, if anything, was happening in a town called Greenwich, B.C. Besides, she probably wanted a bath and some clean clothes more than she wanted international secrets; she'd probably had enough of those. I wondered if I would ever see her again.

Far out there, the white boat changed position in the water. The stem rose, the bow settled, and spray ceased to fly. I was aware that Commander Howland had returned to stand over me.

"He's cut the power," I said. "He's stopping."

"Excuse me. May I look?"

I got up and brushed myself off. Instinctively I looked skyward, but I couldn't see any planes. There probably was at least one up there, however. Whatever kind of a trap it was they were setting, they wouldn't rely entirely on shore-based observation. I heard Howland draw a sharp breath, and looked down. He was beckoning me to the scope.

"Take a look," he whispered, as if he could be heard out there, miles at sea. "Take a good look, fella. There's a sight you won't see often. Not outside a top secret Soviet shipyard. One of their latest and best, and we've got her. We've got her in the bag!"

I lay down again, and got the white boat sharp in

the powerful telescope. I saw that it wasn't alone in the gathering dark. Beyond it lay a great, low, black, wet, monstrous shape. It used to be that automobiles looked like carriages without horses, and submarines looked like real ships that might just duck under the surface occasionally, but this was no ship. It was obviously a creature of the deeps. It was bigger than any pig-boat I'd ever seen, and faster, too. It had been still only a moment; now it was shooting ahead and slipping back under the sea. A moment later it was gone.

"She's down," I reported. Then I said, "Muir's boat seems to be sinking."

"Yes. He'd have opened the sea cocks before he abandoned her."

Howland's voice had a preoccupied sound. I looked up and he was watching, not the sea, but the fancy wrist-chronometer he was wearing. Muir's boat settled slowly and sank stern first. There was nothing left to see out there. I got up and stood beside the commander. I saw his lips move.

"Now," he whispered. *"Now!"*

Nothing happened for a long breath of time. Then a white spot grew on the dark ocean far out there, and out of the middle rose a tremendous geyser of churned-up water. In this water were chunks of black debris. By the time the sound of the explosion reached us, everything was starting to settle back. Presently there was only a widening ring of oily, disturbed water out there. I heard Howland make a funny little sound, and looked at him again. He swallowed oddly, and cleared his throat, and swallowed again.

He said, "Damn, I hate to see a ship die, even one of theirs. You haven't seen anything, of course."

"No, sir."

"If you did see something, it was an accident. A terrible, unexplained accident. Expressions of sympathy will be sent to Moscow, you may be sure, as soon as the local people establish just what it was that blew up in their front yard."

I said, "I don't suppose this has anything to do with the U.S. missile sub that went down on patrol a while back. It couldn't be that our friends tried a bluff of some kind way down in the ocean depths, and we've just given them the only kind of answer they understand?"

He looked at me for a moment. Then he said softly, "Let us hope it was a bluff, Mr. Helm. And let us hope and pray they understand the answer, and believe we mean it, as we do. And of course I have no idea what you are talking about, none at all."

Back in Washington, the consensus seemed to be that old Helm had lucked out as usual. At least that was the attitude I sensed in a certain office on the second floor of a certain old building, never mind where.

"Everyone seems quite satisfied with your performance, Eric," Mac said. "However—"

"Yes, sir," I said.

He hesitated. "Never mind. There is a gentleman named Johnston in town. You will see him tomorrow and tell him whatever seems advisable. Let us try to keep our colleagues happy."

"Happy," I said. "Yes, sir."

"And I have a message for you. A lady wants to see you at the bar at the Hotel Vance at five-thirty this evening."

"Any particular lady?" I asked.

"She said to tell you that Penelope was safe. I gather she wishes to express her gratitude."

I almost didn't recognize her. I don't suppose I was really expecting to find a disheveled young woman in a dirty blue jumper, after the days that had passed, but I wasn't prepared for the extent of the transformation. She was wearing something emerald-green and slinky and Chinese-looking, and the freckles were kind of subdued but the thick hair was a shade or two redder than I remembered, very soft and smooth and bright.

"Mrs. Drilling, ma'am," I said.

She turned from the bar and smiled. I'd forgotten what a pretty woman she really was. "And just what do I call you, Mr. Government Man," she asked. "What is your name today?"

I said, "Looking like that, you don't have to call any man by name, Irish. Just snap your fingers."

She laughed, and stopped laughing. "Penny's all right," she said seriously.

"I know. I got your message."

"She's with her father. I don't know how it's all going

to work out, but in the meantime—" She hesitated. She seemed a little embarrassed. She said rather stiffly, "I pay my debts, Dave."

"Meaning what?"

"We had a… an arrangement, remember? But the payoff was kind of interrupted. Well, you were in my corner when I needed you. You were cruel and ruthless, but I guess you had to be. You accomplished something I couldn't have." She hesitated. "What I mean is, you did your part. I'll do mine. If you're still interested."

I looked at her for a moment. Then I signaled a bartender to bring me a martini. I looked back to Jenny, who was watching me, waiting.

I said, very carefully, "You had an arrangement with a shady private dick named Clevenger, who no longer exists."

A little frowning crease showed between her eyes. "In other words, you aren't interested."

"I didn't say that, Irish. I just mean that you're under no obligations because of what you may have promised a fictitious character in a moment of stress."

She said, rather coolly, "Aren't you being overly honorable?"

I said, "Hell, I'm just setting the record straight. Nobody owes nobody nothing."

After a moment she smiled slowly. "Yes. I see what you mean. It *is* better that way, isn't it?"

She was right. It was.

ABOUT THE AUTHOR

Donald Hamilton was the creator of secret agent Matt Helm, star of 27 novels that have sold more than 20 million copies worldwide.

Born in Sweden, he emigrated to the United States and studied at the University of Chicago. During the Second World War he served in the United States Naval Reserve, and in 1941 he married Kathleen Stick, with whom he had four children.

The first Matt Helm book, *Death of a Citizen*, was published in 1960 to great acclaim, and four of the subsequent novels were made into motion pictures. Hamilton was also the author of several outstanding stand-alone thrillers and westerns, including two novels adapted for the big screen as *The Big Country* and *The Violent Men*.

Donald Hamilton died in 2006.

ALSO AVAILABLE FROM TITAN BOOKS

PRAISE FOR DONALD HAMILTON

"Donald Hamilton has brought to the spy novel
the authentic hard realism of Dashiell Hammett;
and his stories are as compelling, and probably
as close to the sordid truth of espionage,
as any now being told."
Anthony Boucher, *The New York Times*

"This series by Donald Hamilton is the top-ranking
American secret agent fare, with its intelligent
protagonist and an author who consistently writes
in high style. Good writing, slick plotting and
stimulating characters, all tartly flavored with wit."
Book Week

"Matt Helm is as credible a man of violence as has
ever figured in the fiction of intrigue."
The New York Sunday Times

"Fast, tightly written, brutal, and very good…"
Milwaukee Journal

TITANBOOKS.COM

3 2953 01174867 2